I0517089

Sloane Wentworth needs a second chance. When her husband dies, she goes from a soccer mom to a single mother in a heartbeat. She makes him a deathbed promise to seek her fortune and a guy named *Joe* on Cape Cod.

Sloane finds herself harassed and hounded by the press over her late husband's white-collar crimes, losing her job, reputation, and friends. She wants an escape. Maybe a Cape Cod visit is just the thing. Unknown, however, is the role Joe plays.

Sloane is no damsel in distress, but her ship is sinking fast. Perhaps Cape Cod's promises and sea winds will blow good fortune her way. She throws caution to the wind and charts a new course. But will the tide carry her and her young son to a safe harbor? Or will they go down with the ship?

Cape Cod Promise
Copyright © 2023 Kathy Kalmar
ISBN: 978-1-4874-3745-9
Cover art by Martine Jardin

Published by eXtasy Books Inc

Look for us online at:
www.eXtasybooks.com

CAPE COD PROMISE
CAPE COD 1

BY

KATHY KALMAR

DEDICATION

To Larry, who gave me my very own second chance to love, more happiness than I could have believed possible, and healed three broken hearts in the process. I swear I can't love you any more than I already do, and the next day proves me wrong. It takes a special man to mend hearts he didn't break and raise children he didn't make. You do that, my love.

In Memoriam With love
To my forever friend, Linda Wilson, whose skills, talents, and belief in me and my work led to this publication and every book I write. Ours is a relationship forged in the fires of pain, loss, love, and laughter. Living without you is very difficult. You'd love this one!
To Ron Wilson, my best bud, whose deep and abiding friendship led me to Cape Cod.

Acknowledgment
For Carolyn Gilbreath, her counsel and encouragement made this a better book. She is my Best Friend Forever.
To my granddaughter Caoilainn for inspiring a chapter hook and suggesting a scene in Chapter Seven.
With great gratitude, I acknowledge Tina Haveman for her great vision and company; Jay Austin, extraordinary Editor in Chief; Debbie Nygaard, editor and wise counsel; Martine Jardin, artist; Bri Vries, assistant to the Editor in Chief.
Special thanks to The Greater Detroit Romance Writers; Ron and Ginger Wilson, who took us all over Cape Cod and introduced us to our special place; Jane Campo for telling me to keep Cape Cod in

the title; and you, my readers.
Lastly to Doug Marple, webmaster, who keeps the social media site
wheels turning. I'm grateful to you all.

PROLOGUE

March 2021

For all intents and purposes, anyone who saw her now would think she was the epitome of grace, competence, and confidence. Indeed, she carefully cultivated just that image, working hard to appear to be a well-put-together woman in charge. Those who saw her would be fooled by her expensive blunt-cut hairdo, classic clothes, poise, and the way she carried herself. However, at this moment, she was not what her appearance suggested—at all. They'd misjudge her stance, seeing it as elegant, even statuesque. Her fraud was a finely crafted façade, and that's deliberate. It gives the impression that the world must be her oyster, but they'd be wrong ... dead wrong.

Inside she was a volcano about ready to explode. Bending low over her husband's gurney, she was afraid and furious.

The thirty-something, one-time healthy-as-a-horse man struggled to speak. "S-So-Sor-ry ... Our p-pl-lan ..."—*cough*—"Cape ... Lonnie, promise meeee ..." —*wheeze*—"find Joe." Each pain-filled word tore from an undoubtedly tortured, raw throat and laboring lungs. *Sigh.* The steam seemed to go out of him.

She heard his words ... could see every syllable was torture, each sound strangled. But down deep in her core, she knew. Knew as she drove him to the hospital with a raging fever and hacking cough. Knew as her body went into shock. Knew when her brain went numb. Knew before her husband

1

rasped his last words . . . *promise me.* He was as good as gone. She felt it in her gut, her soul, and in the huge hole that rent through the fabric of who she was.

The hospitalist's voice droned on in the background. "Squawk, squawk, squawk, blah, blah, blah." The voice sounded like Charlie Brown's teacher.

She couldn't comprehend it. Fear was driving her insane. *All he had to do was take the jab.*

The hospital said she couldn't stay. She walked out as an orderly wheeled her husband away to admit him into the Intensive Care Unit alongside so many others.

PART ONE

Genesis 2011

Chapter One: Up, up and Away

Labor Day Weekend, Saturday afternoon, 2011

"Ready to get high?" Seth grinned and shook his head, biting back a wolf whistle. His smile grew as he watched the willowy Sloane Somersan join him. She was a fox, looking hot in her crop top and barely there, shredded denim cutoff shorts. He could see the pockets peeking below the miniscule hemline, knowing they couldn't even hold a tissue.

"Always," Sloane replied in a dry tone. "By the way, your play on words is way lame."

Seth held back a laugh. Sloane was all business but threw him an *are-you-kidding-me* look as she climbed into the cockpit of his twin-engine Piper Cherokee 140. She withdrew her medical certificate and logbook from her crossbody bag, stowed the purse, and began inspecting the cockpit instruments as required by the preflight checklist. He nodded. Sloane had always disagreed with checking the cockpit first, believing a walkaround should be first and then the cockpit check.

He grinned. "Are we ready to roll?"

She sent him a look of disgust. "Only in your dreams, Captain F-P—"

"F-P?"

She inclined her head toward him, batting her eyelashes. "Flight Police. You're policing me to see if I'm following the stupid preflight checklist, and as you can see, I am—even if it doesn't make sense. More importantly, it's inefficient."

4

He looked her in the eye, cocked his head, then very deliberately batted *his* eyelashes and winked — at her. "Their circus, their monkeys."

She shrugged. "So, monkey see, monkey do. Capisce."

Seth underscored his small win with a grin. "To answer your question, no, I'm not air traffic control. I'm just *your* everyday flight *instructor* doing my *job*. Making sure you do yours — correctly."

Sloane responded with an airy tone and a wave of her hand. "Don't mind me, I'll just continue to conduct the *prescribed* preflight inspections as, uh, as prescribed." Her gaze swept over the control panel again, checking the instruments, pedals, gauges, switches, and other flight controls. "Cockpit check complete."

Seth followed Sloane out of the plane to verify her observations. She proceeded with her walkaround, checking everything on the aircraft from the nose to the tail per the prescribed checklist. Then she nodded her satisfaction with her inspection, proving she knew her stuff. In short, she executed the walkaround — precisely — as the instructions required.

She turned to him with a smile and declared her inspection complete. "You're not getting rid of me — aka flunking me — that easily. This bird is flightworthy."

Seth responded with his own smile. "Affirmed check complete."

With a tilt of her head, she said, "Now, we're ready to roll, Commander."

They boarded the aircraft again, and Sloane prepared for takeoff going through the required maneuvers. She scanned the terrain to see if any other flights were arriving or departing. "Visual check complete." She initiated the departure sequence, providing the squawk code. "Ground, Cherokee 3339, at small tower, request taxi and go, runway 33 left."

Ground control replied, "Cherokee 3339, proceed runway

33 left, hold for takeoff."

Sloane began to taxi toward the runway, parking at the end of the run and awaiting clearance. "Ground, Cherokee 3339, runway 33 left, holding for takeoff."

Seconds later, Ground came through. "Cherokee 3339, runway 33 left, cleared for takeoff."

Even though Seth was Sloane's flight instructor, supervising her through takeoffs and landings and guiding her through the maneuvers in the air, she always seemed to chaff at his supervision. Clearly chomping at the bit, she revealed her eagerness to soar solo.

As he walked her through the steps for takeoff, he had to smother an admiring smile and tamp down the rise in his groin. But he would have had to be born blind not to notice the rigid set of her jaw as if counting to ten in her head. Her smooth even features betrayed nothing—much—but she had a tell, a tiny tic. If not for that, he might not have noticed her irritation. *Sloane, so ready, poised to soar. Wonder if she'd be that eager to fly into my bed.*

He cleared his throat. "You got this, Sloane."

Sloane said nothing, stoically keeping her focus on the flight, not him. He didn't like that . . . wasn't used to it. Normally female students developed crushes on him. Nothing that lasted and nothing he pursued until after they were no longer a potential sexual harassment lawsuit. He liked his independence. Didn't want to be tied down. *Keep it fluid.*

"You'll be flying solo soon. But for now, keep in mind that I'm ultimately responsible for this flight. For you." He repeated that, although he'd said it several times before.

"Whatever. I get it. I hear you. Yadda, yadda, yadda," she said, confirming his earlier thoughts.

As Sloane followed the flight plan, Seth led her through several routine procedures—simple straight-and-level flying and the climb-descent processes. Sloane had already mastered the go-around maneuver, which in his opinion, was a must-know procedure. Then he upped the ante leading her through a more challenging set of performance exercises involving maneuver planning, situational awareness, as well as division, diversion, and focus of attention. Any weakness in execution would likely be due to her lack of understanding, her deficiency of fundamental skills, or his failure to instruct sufficiently. However, he knew she was adept in those areas. Sloane was set to fly solo for sure.

She sure lifts me. He glanced at his crotch and mentally groaned. *Keep it professional, buddy. She's your student.*

Sloane had been doing great, so Seth decided to show her a new maneuver. Each time he introduced something new, he usually broke it into easy-to-learn chunks, but this time, he felt she was beyond ready for more. He had witnessed increased smoothness in her flight control applications, and she demonstrated a higher ability to sense the airplane's altitude and orientation.

"Okay. Today we're mixing things up. Ready?"

She grinned. "Aye, aye, Capitán."

He laughed. "Wrong lingo. Right attitude. New terrain, new maneuver. This one is called the sleep turn maneuver. It's not a shallow bank angle turn like we usually perform. It's steeper. It calls for pitch control pressures, added power for lift, altitude adjustments, and more airspeed. First, scan for any hazards."

"Hazards? Say what?"

He nodded. "As in geese, wind, other planes, drones, intrusions—"

"Intrusions?"

He laughed, "Alien crafts."

Sloane cocked an eyebrow in his direction. "Roger that."

"Remember what I taught you about over-banking. Avoid that and watch your lift."

He took over the controls to demonstrate. He loved this

maneuver and hoped Sloane would, too. Judging by how her lower lip ticked, he figured the flush in her cheeks must be excitement and anticipation, not fear. "Baby steps?"

"Hell no. Let me try."

He guided her through the first steps and helped her finish. By the end, she positively glowed, clearly excited by the thrill of the turn, the lure of possible danger. She seemed almost giddy, and so was he.

He felt the rush of something else, too. More than a surge of adrenaline could explain. It had to do with Sloane, with delight, not the flight.

Seth struggled to keep to the instructor-trainee relationship, but it was challenging. Not just because she was a beautiful distraction but also because she was so damned good, competent, and capable. He found her competence sexy.

Sloan executed the lesson apparently fearlessly, nearly flawlessly. With the maneuver completed, she leveled out—gradually reducing altitude—perfectly positioning the aircraft, and they soon reached the threshold for landing.

Seth noted Sloane always handled the hardest parts of the exercises—takeoffs and landings—with little outward sign of nerves and a shipload of skill. She executed a great solid landing again and began performing the post-flight shutdown. He assisted, and when the plane was secured, she prepared to leave, but not before she completed the exit walkaround checking the aircraft for damage. *Like I taught her.*

Seth loathed letting her go, but it wasn't professional to ask a student out. But soon it wouldn't be a problem. What he could do, however, was ask, "Got plans for this holiday weekend?" He strived for an offhand tone and casual manner.

She giggled. "I got high. Isn't that enough?"

He ached, imagining another type of high she could equally enjoy. Not one from flying or drugs either. "There's a big party tonight."

She laughed. "It's the weekend. There's always a party. Plus, as you pointed out, it's summer's last hurrah. Nothing else is high on my wish list. Not after the high of flying."

"This party is at the Delta Omicron Omega Lake House, the party of the century, guaranteed to be epic. You a *go* for that?"

"Possibly . . ."

Seth was some years older than Sloane, and as her flight instructor, he felt protective despite his sometimes-obvious interest. Partying could be risky, and she was a real rookie if he ever saw one. Someone needed to keep an eye out for her. Why not him? "I have connections. I can get you in. A group of us are going. It's a good way to sample the scene, see the sights out there, get your feet wet, learn the ropes, like you say, yadda, yadda. Best to start by being with someone you can trust. I'll be there. You'd be in good hands."

"Said the spider to the fly," Sloane replied in a dry tone.

He paused, forming a good response. "No, not like a spider. Like Superman."

"Huh?"

He looked her in the eye. "I cannot tell a lie."

"Who are you? George Washington? Appears you have your history books mixed up with your comics books."

Seth flashed a sly smile. "Au Contraire. One of Superman's superpowers is honesty. He can't lie. It's biologically impossible."

"Biologically, huh? Does an alert sound when he's about to fib? "

Seth crossed his heart. "Hope to die if I ever tell a lie. You're smart to be skeptical, though." He cocked a glance her way. "To be afraid."

Sloane bristled. "As if. Do I look scared? I can deal. I may be a rookie *pilot*, but I know how to *partay*." Her lip ticked.

"Even spunky, *experienced* Lois Lane took risks and copped a free flight when offered one. I'm the designated driver for the night—you know, keeping everyone safe and alive."

She grinned. "Haven't I already proven myself? My smooth landing shows competence and experience."

"Think abooout it." He drew out the statement like a member of the Mafia. "How 'bout I swing by, and we'll see? Bring whatshername."

Seth walked Sloane to her bike.

She looked over her shoulder and hesitated. "Addie? My roommate? She's going to the fireworks with some friends. I'm invited too, sooo, I dunno." She smiled, mounted her bike, and gave a little flighty dance of her fingers as she waved over her shoulder. "Ta-Ta."

"Ta-Ta." *Wait. What kind of goodbye is* Ta-Ta? *Talk about lame.*

Sloane reviewed her option as she biked home from the Ann Arbor Municipal Airport. Fireworks? Party with Seth? Hmm, Seth was hot. Hot trumped a trip to Beacon Hill. According to those in the know, Delta Omicron Omega pledges weren't as pressured to engage in the usual asinine antics. The fraternity had a low incident rate. Seth would be around, so the invitation promised to be an acceptable risk.

The Lake House *party* didn't interest Sloane much, but the *mansion* did. It was on her bucket list and one of the reasons she chose this university to study. As an art and architecture major, the structure was a huge draw. Once the home of a baron of business, the opportunity to see it up close and personal made the party tempting.

The house was featured in the *Architectural Digest,* built at the height of the Gilded Era, and seriously retro. To top all that off, it perched on a hill with a wide sloping lawn overlooking the lake. *Here's my chance to get inside . . . roam around a little.* It'd be an experience she might not otherwise get. Precious few fraternity parties were held there. *Maybe I should reconsider . . .*

When she reached her dorm, the sun was setting, coloring the sky in a blend of hues as reds, golds, and blues bled through the clouds. She entered her suite and spotted Addie's note sitting on top of the pizza box lid that said, *Left for fireworks. Chill at Beacon Hill.*

The room darkened as night fell. The only light was from fireflies outside the window. Sloane turned on the closest lamp, scarfed down the pizza, then headed for the shower. The evening was sticky and humid, and the shower steam fogged the mirror, leaving her feeling damp and clammy. She'd dress light for the night regardless of either event, opting for a fashionable asymmetrical top, skimpy bra, and a short denim skirt. She completed the look by shoving her feet into comfortable cowboy boots. She was good to go. *Fireworks or Lake House Party?*

Her phone pinged. She checked it to find a text from Seth.

Ready 2 rumble 2night?

Without hesitation, she replied.

K.

C U @ 10

She sent him a party hat emoji.

11

CHAPTER TWO: I GOTTA GET OUTTA THIS PLACE

Saturday evening

Sloane smiled when Seth arrived promptly at 10 o'clock. As promised, he occupied the driver's seat. She squeezed into the back seat of his Ford F-150 XLT 4x4 Crew Cab Pickup with a smile, slightly hunched between an eclectic assortment of people. The group was a blend of friends representing undergrads to graduates, including both sexes.

Seth made a round of quick introductions. He nodded to the girl crammed in next to her. "This is my sis, Mallory. Stick close together, you two."

Sloane managed a cramped wave, chaffing at the directive, her lower lip ticking. *Who does he think he is? My social flight controller, my handler? I don't think so. I don't need a babysitter.*

Mallory didn't look like she wanted to be saddled with Sloane either. Both turned toward Seth and scowled. Mallory even stuck her tongue out at her brother, then caught Sloane's gaze and winked. Sloane knew they were *good* and gave Mallory a thumbs up.

The drive to the lake went faster than Sloane expected. A wide variety of vehicles—several lanes deep—forced Seth to search for parking alongside and down the road. "Damn, it wasn't supposed to be so huge." He put the truck into idle, so the group could get out and join the party.

Sloane slipped out, wagging her fingers in her signature

Ta-Ta gesture. "Catch you later." She crossed the road, weaving through the parked cars to get to the festivities. Mallory seemed to melt away into the crowd.

Bright strings of Christmas lights lined the perimeter of the grounds stretching from the house down the four-hundred-foot sloping lawn to the beach. Sloane could see partiers milling down by the shore, their bodies backlit by the light of the moon and tiki torches. Moonlight cut a perfect swath of pearly shine across the lake's smooth surface, giving the night potential, promise, and possibility. The beach could become a peaceful and ideal place for lovers and skinny dipping, except for the huge bonfire . . . and a keg to boot. Sloane's antennae detected an underlying pulse that defied the placidity of the moonscape. Alcohol appeared to be flowing freely.

The music had a wild vibe, and the crowd responded. Its tempo increased as the music blared, the beat pulsing through the alcohol-fueled ensemble. In a heartbeat, raucous horseplay broke out, beckoning a rowdier bunch. Firecrackers exploded, adding to the din. Sloane steered clear of that scene and headed toward the lakefront house.

She worked her way through the people milling around the back of the house, and someone pressed a foaming red plastic cup into her hands. Apparently, everyone had a drink. A few guys had one in each hand, guzzling from both. She expected the foamy drink to be beer, but it wasn't. She had yet to cultivate a taste for the yeasty brew. Instead, it was, in her opinion, an upgrade, a frothy, fruity, liquor cocktail thingy — way better than beer. Sloane giggled and thought of Addie, hoping her friend was enjoying the Labor Day fireworks. That event wasn't likely to have pot wafting in the air.

Sloane noticed the closer she got to the house, the more the scent of pot hung in the breezeless night. While this wasn't her first party, pot fumes this early made her wonder about the air inside the home. She inhaled deeply, enjoying the free buzz.

People nudged her, pushing her body here, there, and everywhere as if she was a rolling computer chair. She looked around for the people she had arrived with, but they had scattered hither and yon. She didn't see Seth anywhere either. Still, her drink was good, the crowd friendly, and she blended in with the others. Katy Perry's song *Firework* started playing in the background, and like most parties, the music was loud, the dancing intense.

She joined the crowd, dancing by herself at first, but it wasn't long before she found others joining her. She was swept away by the tide of people shuffling around her and stumbled. Her head began spinning. Her balance was off, her steps uncertain. The drink and the crowds had her listing to the left.

Sloane finally got herself to the mansion. The structure reminded her of the castle in Downton Abbey. Or perhaps part of it suggested Marie Antoinette's Petit Trianon. The lake house was certainly as stately and solid as Antoinette's. To enter, she navigated a set of limestone stairs leading up to a wide porch. The beautiful wrought-iron grillwork-on-glass doors opened to a spacious, pristine, stone entryway and large foyer. Standing sentry to two reception rooms were beautiful Italian limestone columns. She could not resist the urge to touch them as she moved along. She was sure the floors she walked were Greek marble—from the same quarry as the Acropolis, no doubt. She had been there, and even as a teen, she had a keen eye for materials and design. What little she'd seen so far made this walkthrough feel like a tour of Europe and its artistry.

The first-floor ceilings were high, airy, and bright with crystal chandeliers. Brocade draperies hung from towering windows. To the far left was a sweeping double marble staircase. She knew the walnut railings had to be French, likely commissioned and crafted in Europe. The home, being from another era, did not have an open-concept floor plan. Clearly, the mansion's interior did not disappoint, and she was glad she had the opportunity to see it up close and in person. After all, the house — not the party within — had been her objective.

Sloane was enchanted. She momentarily imagined herself in another land, a similar place, decades earlier, where she would be garbed in satin or silk. Perhaps a foxtail stole would lay across her shoulder with long pearls gracing her neck. A fashionable cigarette holder between her fingers — not to smoke but for appearances.

She reached a stairway blocked by a velvet rope. She was hot and woozy from the crowd crammed around her. *I need space to breathe.* To escape the press of partiers, she ducked beneath the rope, seizing the opportunity to dash up the stairs.

Upstairs, a long hall swept the expanse barely lit by well-spaced low-light sconces. The corridor had doors lining both sides. Most were closed and dark, but down a way, soft light spilled from a room left invitingly open. She crept in and found it fully occupied.

The occupants were otherwise engaged and didn't notice her. Naked coupling bodies were entwined on every available surface — filling the spacious room and its alcoves and nooks. The sight gave her a jolt. Shocked beyond belief, she backed away as quickly as she could only to plow into a body — a taller, broader male — whose hands wandered freely.

The guy's hot breath reeked of hard liquor. "Whas yer hurry, hon? This whatcha lookin' for?" His hands groped her.

She spun away, pitching her drink in his face and pushing at his eager hands. "Get offa me!" She drove her knee — hard — into his crotch.

He released her, groaning and muttering, "Biiitch!"

Her chest heaving and freed from his grasp, she darted away and stumbled upon a much narrower set of stairs.

Whew. She raced downstairs and entered what might have been a pantry. It led into a keg haven at the back of the spacious, functional kitchen at odds with the beauty and grandeur of the stately building. She saw a row of bottles—soft drinks and juices—with a lot of hard liquor on a large table that served as a bar. That explained the concoction she had been drinking. She grabbed a foaming cup with trembling hands, not caring if it was beer or not. She chugged it, spilling some in her haste. Dropping the cup, she swiped her hand across her lips, struggling to compose herself and deal with the mess.

She pushed her way through the crowd, realizing others had breached the velvet ropes, too, mingling freely in the finely appointed adjoining rooms. No longer interested in the house or its bones, she pushed through the crowd and hurried outside.

She snagged a drink from a guy who sported a trayful and spotted several other servers bearing trays of canapes and finger foods. She shook her head at the paradox the party revealed, a confusing mixture of a swanky event and a wild keg party.

The tempo of the music and the people sucked her into the party's vortex. Periodically, she sipped her drink. The last days of summer were sticky, muggy, and hot—like this party. She found it hard to navigate as she was jostled around. She, too, was hot and tipsy. *Already? What the hell?*

More than once, Sloane found herself stumbling, either engulfed or swept away by the tide of people. Her head began spinning when a guy careened into her spilling the plastic cup's contents on her shirt.

He made vain attempts to apologize while ineffectually swiping at it to clean it off. "Sorry 'bout that." He grabbed her by the hand and pulled her through the maze of partiers. "Gotta get the shirt offa ya. You're dripping wet." The guy introduced himself as Chad. He found a lone hoodie on a chair and gave it to her.

She felt conflicted, not sure if she should kick or kiss him, laugh, or cry. She turned her back, whipped off the clingy, sticky, wet top, and attempted to don the hoodie.

Someone grabbed it away before she could pull it on.

Several jocks played *Monkey in the Middle* with the hoodie as Sloane scrambled to grab it to cover herself and the scrap of lace that was her bra.

This caught the crowd's attention, and a chant began, "Off! Off! Off! Off! Strip it!" to the cadence of *We Will Rock You*, by Queen.

Another coed might go with the flow, but Sloane was not that someone. Why had she thought a flimsy bra was a good idea? This was *so* not the time to be a good sport. She was not just getting her feet wet like Captain Superman promised. *So much for Superman when I need 'im.*

A boozy frat bro thought it'd be a good idea to toss *Sloane* instead, and she found herself flying—not in a plane this time—but through a half dozen burly arms. She was slammed into someone, which had her head spinning.

A voice bellowed. "That's enough. Find something else to do. This is over. Put. Her. Down."

The crowd booed, but the free-for-all broke up.

On shaky feet again, Sloane breathed a sigh of relief and automatically followed the voice amid the crowds' cries.

"Spoil Sport."

"Downer."

"Party Pooper."

Emboldened by her escape, Sloane looked over her shoulder and yelled, "Dickheads."

Once out of the fray and back by the bay, now the peaceful place it first promised, she stopped to face and thank her ally. A scowl crossed Seth's face, and he didn't appear impressed with her.

Sloane gulped. *How embarrassing. Damn.*

She swore she could smell the smoke pouring out his ears.

"What do you think you're doing?" he growled.

Upset with herself and his tone, she felt a mix of glad, sad, and mad all at the same time. Her voice shook with her churning emotions, but she managed to squeak, "Dancing. Partying."

"Dancing? That's what you call it? What's this?" He looked at the cup that she somehow held onto.

Huh? Where'd that come from? "Geez, I don't know. Duh, my drink."

He took it. "Where'd you get it?"

"Whaa?" She might have slurred a bit. "Is this the Spanish Inquisition? Chad gave it to me. Maybe?"

"Oh, that explains everything." Seth sneered, obviously peeved." Don't you know who Chad is? That cad's known to lace drinks—"

Sloane giggled. "Chad . . . cad . . . Thas funny. It rhymes."

"—with drugs." Seth dumped the drink on the ground. "Always get, or better yet, bring your own alcohol from now on." He cocked his head. "Are you even twenty-one?"

Sloane ignored his question, biting back a sharp *none of your beeswax*. She suddenly felt weak and woozy. She stared at him blankly and swayed.

Seth caught her in his arms.

She clung to him like *Saran Wrap. He looks so hot when he's mad.*

He struggled to untangle them, but Sloane made that very difficult, especially since she was literally falling all over him.

"Where was I?" he grumbled.

She laughed. *Everything Seth says is so hilarious.*

Seth continued. "Don't set your drink down even for a second. Ever. You're lucky you're still standing. God only knows what Chad planned to do with you. Ever heard of Gamma-hydroxybutyrate, sometimes called *liquid ecstasy . . .* or

Rohypnol, also known as *roofies*? Even Ambien can be used . . ."

Sloane's blank look must have made Seth shift gears.

"Let's get you out of here." He took her elbow and marched her away.

But Sloane was in no such hurry. Her latent, barely acknowledged feelings for Seth suddenly flowed through her bloodstream with a vengeance. She glommed onto him, wrapping herself around him—tight. *He feels so good, and I'm seriously horny.*

Seth unwound her, then tried to walk and support her sagging body, but she made that difficult. When they arrived at his truck, he maneuvered her inside, reaching across her body to fasten the seatbelt. His lips brushed across her cheek as he straightened up.

Sloane raised her lips and caught his in a kiss, entwining her fingers in his hair. "Mmm," The moan escaped her, making him jolt away.

"There's more where that came from." Sloane trailed her fingers across his lips while her other hand strayed to his zipper pull. "Come to Mama."

Seth pushed her hands away, closed her door, and ran around to the driver's side. His hands shook when he pressed the ignition.

Sloane leaned into his sturdy, well-muscled frame and resumed trailing her fingers up his arms.

Seth stiffened and growled. "Stop. I'm driving! "

Her hand strayed to his lap again, dancing her fingers over his package.

He jerked the wheel. "Damn, woman. Slow down. I mean, cut it out."

"Sure." She fiddled with his zipper to continue her teasing.

His hand crushed hers. "Enough."

"I aim to please. I can feel you want me."

"You're high. Quit it."

The car lurched off the road. Seth stopped the truck, stomped to her side, and yanked her out. Sloane leaned into him, still trying to mess with him. He lost his balance, they tumbled to the ground, and she landed on top of him. She wasn't wearing much at all and again felt the evidence of his interest.

Seth shoved Sloane off and dragged her to her feet. She swayed, so he grabbed her arm to steady her, and she tried to lean into him again. He huffed in frustration and hefted her over his shoulder in a fireman's carry. Luckily, he knew exactly where he was and walked the short distance to his family's cottage. He unlocked the door and carried her inside over the threshold.

Sloane squirmed around until he had to shift his hold to carry her princess-style.

She giggled. "I do. Kiss the bride. Wanna do me?"

"Not the time to ask," he muttered, setting her on her feet.

She swayed again. "Don't ya want me, baby?"

"Not this way, I don't. Stop."

What little clothing she wore hung in shreds, practically falling off her. She slid out of them and then tried to remove his clothes. When that failed, she slid her hands underneath the waist of his pants and tried to grope him.

"No." He fought her onslaught and hauled her to the bathroom. He turned the shower on and dragged her in—struggling—still wearing all his clothes.

She crooned. "Yes, baby, yes. That's what I'm talking about. Let's get you naked, too."

With force, he looked her straight in the eye. "Not. Gonna. Happen. No."

She made another weak attempt to grab his belt, but he managed to direct the cold spray on her, hoping to sober her up. But the combination of drugs, shock, and icy water apparently had the opposite effect. She keeled over and was out like a light.

Seth was fit to be tied, his patience running thin as he fought to control his hormones. This situation had turned as bad as a stalled-engine flight, and he was getting nowhere close to where he wanted it to be. Sloane had crashed, and he needed to find a way to soften her landing.

He shook his head, hefted her out of the bathtub, and dumped her, naked, in the nearest bed. Unfortunately, it was his. He blotted her off with the sheet and yanked the blanket over her. Then he stepped out of his clothes, leaving them in a damp heap where they fell, and returned to the shower. He stared at himself as the cold water failed to dampen the flames the sight of her naked body lit.

"Nice," he muttered. "Just what I frickin' need. A naked coed in my bed and a hard-on I can't control."

Sometimes it sucked having a conscience and being a decent man. *I seriously suck at being Superman.* He dried himself off, threw on some dry jeans and a shirt he didn't bother to button, and headed back to the party. He was the effin' designated driver, for Christopher's sake.

CHAPTER THREE: THE SOUNDS OF SILENCE

Sunday morning

Sloane woke slowly, opening one eye cautiously to look around. *Where am I?* The covers over her were smothering, so she shoved them off. She pushed the hair out of her face and propped her head on her elbow. She felt woozy but struggled to sit up. She failed, the motion making her head spin and her stomach rebel. She hung her head over the edge of the bed and realized she was naked. *What the hell? Why am I naked? What's happening?*

Suddenly, snatches of events raced across her mind like they were projected on a screen. She moaned and hung her head while disjointed images and sounds paraded by.

A bonfire. Music.

Yummy drink.

Flying. Lust. Noise. Seth.

Seth? There seems to be a hole in my memory. What the heck happened?

Bouncing. Hard arms. Loud shouts. Desire. Lights flickering. Heat. Superman.

Superman?

Skinny-dipping.

Huh. Did I really go skinny-dipping? Naked?

Chanting. Crowds pushing. Lurching. Stumbling. Chad. Her clothes shredding.

Where is Superman? Exploding firecrackers? Gunshot?

Car?

I don't know what the hell happened. Was I raped? Did I seduce someone?

Crawling all over Seth. Grabbing Seth's groin. Not. Gonna. Happen.

Sloane groaned. *What in God's name happened?* She shook her head, trying in vain to clear it, but things remained foggy, and she felt nauseous, not hung over. *What's wrong with me?*

She heaved, her stomach choosing that moment to rebel in a major way.

She crawled out of bed and inched forward, trying to hold back her vomit. She failed. Merely moving was a total struggle. She reached the porcelain throne and emptied her belly . . . she hoped. Bitter bile bit her tongue and tortured her raw throat. She clutched the fabric nearest her, trying to wipe her mouth and cover herself. *Yuck.* Her stomach heaved again. She huddled into the fetal position on the floor, unable to stop shaking. She was a hot mess. Tears ran down her face. Her head was pounding, and the pulses at her temple throbbed. She was sick, wrung out, and very confused. She stayed where she was while the room swirled.

Sometime later, Sloane heard a slamming door and footsteps. *What the hell?* The floorboards groaned under the weight of heavy steps.

"Sloane!"

She knew that voice. *Is it Chad? Seth?* At the thought, she wretched and heaved again. And again. *Just kill me now.* She shut her eyes.

She suddenly felt hot breath against her cheek and squeezed her lids tighter, afraid to trust the low soothing nonsense words pouring softly from someone's lips. She shuddered and felt gentle hands rubbing her back. Instinct led her to lean toward the source of the soft, comforting touch. *Addie? Aftershave? Undoubtedly male. Not Addie. Definitely. Not. Addie.*

She kept her eyes closed, afraid to know for sure. The door opened. The breeze chilled her.

A female voice yelled in a high-pitched screech, "What's going on here?"

The figure holding her jumped up, dropping her not so gently, adding insult to injury. "It's not what you think."

The female wasn't having it. "No, then what is it? She's naked, and you're here. Why? Oh, and did I mention she's naked."

Before the dude could answer, the female went on. "What the hell is Sloane doing here to begin with?"

Full-on miserable, Sloane struggled to hold back the scream building in her throat. Try as she may, her soul-wrenching cry echoed in the marble-tiled room, and she shivered uncontrollably.

The deep voice said, "Look, she's been drugged—"

"Drugged? What?"

"Doesn't matter how or why she's here. Run the damn tub. We've got to get her warm and clean her up."

Feet scurried, and water ran in the tub full blast.

The male lifted her and carefully set her into the warm cocoon of the bathtub. Once he got her situated, he spoke. "Oh, be careful where you walk. She's been puking."

The female apparently stepped into the slop and slid. "Now you tell me," she grumbled. "I'll take care of her. Get my sweats from my room, and for God's sake, get out of here. No woman wants to be seen like this. Make yourself useful."

"I'm trying to be, Mal. Give me a break."

Mal? The female voice belonged to Mallory?

Sloane felt Mallory's gentle hands help her lean backward until her shoulders rested against the tub. "Slide down. Let the water wash over your head. Relax. We got you."

Sloane started to comply but raised up when the word *we* registered. *Who's we? Where am I? Is Seth here? Is the man Chad or Seth? Why can't I remember? What's wrong with me?*

Mallory pushed her gently back into the warm water. "Everything's fine. You're safe. Let's just get you cleaned up, okay?"

Sloane slowly opened her eyes. She felt wounded to her core. Violated. She shook so hard she created mini waves in the tub water. After she was out and into Mallory's warm sweats, a knock sounded on the door.

"Tea's ready," the male said through the door.

Sloane figured she must look as green as she felt when Mallory shouted, "Hell with that shit. Get her some ginger ale instead. Tea won't help."

"Yes, ma'am." Footsteps receded and returned quickly, followed by a soft knock.

Mallory retrieved the pop that slipped through the barely opened doorway.

Sloane grimaced at the thought of adding anything to her stomach. It hurt from all the retching.

Gratefully and avoiding eye contact, Sloane sipped the soda, praying the carbonated ginger did the trick. Mercifully, her stomach settled a few moments later. She no longer felt sick — unless a raging headache counted.

Mallory led her to the living room and helped her sit on the sofa. Malory wrapped a throw over her. Sloane looked up to see Seth sitting across from her. Utter embarrassment washed over her.

Seth fidgeted, head bowed, his fingers laced as he muttered, "I'm so sorry —"

"Save it. All I want is a ride home. I don't want to talk about this. Ever."

He started again. "All that, it's on me —"

Again, Sloane cut him off with a raised hand. She was beyond mortified. Preferring not to see his face, let alone look him in the eye, she turned toward Mallory. "Thanks for the clothes. Can you get me back to my dorm?"

Mallory nodded. "No problem."

Only then did she look at Seth. "All I need from you is your sister. From here on out, mind your own damn knittin'."

Seth stood. "I'll drive you. I got you here. I'll get you home."

"Mallory's fine. I'd rather ride with her."

Seth sighed and sat back down. "Just let me explain . . . Sometimes rejection is protection. Drugs make people over-sexualized — "

She cut him off this time with a look that nailed him to the chair he occupied. "I've heard all I want to hear. Leave it, and me, be. *Please.*"

Sloane returned to the bedroom to retrieve what was left of her clothes, trying vainly not to fall apart. Head down, deliberately not making any further contact, she hurried outside to climb into the car Mallory led her to and fastened the seatbelt.

Mallory cleared her throat. "I owe you an apology. I should have stayed with you. The way Seth said."

"Hell, Seth said a lot of things. Some Superman."

"Huh?"

"Never mind. I don't want to discuss it with you either. I'm beyond humiliated. Can your sympathy. I just want to get out of here. The sooner, the better."

Mallory cast her a sideway glance, then hit the accelerator to comply.

When they arrived, Sloane murmured her thanks, averting her eyes. "I'll get your sweats back to you."

"No worries. If you want to talk — "

"I never want to talk about it again . . . with you, with anyone. Thanks for the ride."

Sloane closed the door intending never to see Mallory or Seth again — ever.

When Sloane reached her dorm suite, Addie — cell phone

26

in hand—rushed to her.

"Where the hell have you been, Sloane? You've got to get home pronto. There's been an accident . . . it's your mom . . . it's bad. I'm so sorry . . ."

Sloane fell to her knees.

PART TWO

Exodus 2021

CHAPTER FOUR: GONE, GONE, GONE

Late July 2021

"Are we there yet?" eight-year-old Joel asked for the umpteenth time.

Sloane Wentworth drew in a deep breath, mustering her patience, and said, "Nope, but we are starting our adventure. We're entering a foreign country! Remember what I told you?"

Her little boy nodded. He didn't shout out and bounce around like he would have in the past. He went mostly silent, his words few and far between since the death of his father . . . her husband. Her once exuberant boy had toned down abruptly. *No use rehashing the past. This is an exciting journey for us, remember?* The light in her son's eyes was something she hadn't seen since . . . well, forever.

Nonetheless, Sloane had to press him. "The border guard will ask you where you live and where we're going. You'll have to answer the questions. If you don't, we'll have to turn around and take the long way down to Ohio, across Pennsylvania to New York, then head north again. So, answer when they ask." She could only hope and pray he would.

Two things she knew she could expect from Joel lately— loud, angry outbursts or periods of profound silence. All she had heard on the trip so far was Joel yelling the dreaded repeated question. She prayed this journey would help her son become the loving child he used to be.

Whitt would not have believed the changes in their son.

29

Sloane rubbed her throbbing temples, praying she wasn't in for yet another debilitating migraine. She was prone to them before, but ever since . . . *Stop. Don't go there.* Migraines nearly leveled her when grief and worry didn't. Each day a flotilla of ever-increasing responsibilities threatened to sink her ship. *Don't think. Don't be negative.*

She shook herself and said, "We're going to cross the border now. Just think, we are going to another country, Canada!"

The Canadian border had just reopened. Travelers could finally enter after a year-long border shutdown. Lines of huge long-haul trucks, cars, and RVs stretched for miles ahead of them, all waiting for passage. Sloane counted at least thirteen lanes of vehicles converging to three. *Shit.* She hoped they wouldn't be detained or delayed further by COVID policies.

As they approached a security booth, Sloane cleared her throat, striving for a mellow yet firm tone. "Have your mask ready, Joel. The border guard may ask where you're going. You remember, right?"

Joel nodded and actually spoke in a normal tone. "To see where Daddy was born. Mass-achoo-zits." He giggled, then demanded, "Say *Gesundheit* cuz I sneezed." He covered his amusement with his Spiderman mask as they pulled up to the booth.

"God bless you." Sloane complied with Joel's demand — or hoped she had.

The border guards had gone on strike after a pay freeze, which further compromised transit into Canada. Sloane prayed for no trouble as they passed through security.

It seemed everyone was tired and tense lately. *Who can blame them? Folks are angry and frustrated, worn down by the pandemic.* Sloane was suffering from her own version of what people called COVID fatigue. She speculated that the little-known phenomenon had morphed into a psychosis that caused people to do bizarre things. She'd heard of people running their cars into houses, even police cars, at incredible speeds and living—no less—only to run away from the scene. Maybe that insanity accounted for the tragedy in her life. *What had Whitt been thinking? Had he suffered a version of COVID psychosis?*

Joel let out a screech just as she lowered the car window. "No! You hafta say *Gesundheit!*" His volume increased dramatically despite his mask.

Sloan shushed him. "The border guard—"

"Say *Gesundheit!*" Joel's voice rose another octave as he yelled, "You hafta say it!"

"Everything all right here?" the guard asked, giving Joel a sharp look.

Sloane tensed and ground out, "Yes. Fine. He's just upset. He made a joke . . ."

The young woman quirked a finely arched brow as if she wasn't buying it. Her tone turned cold. "What is your purpose in Canada?"

Sloane strived for calm, still off balance by Joel's outburst and the guard's attitude, and answered, "Passing through. Going to Cape Cod via Canada." She turned to Joel. "*Gesundheit.*"

Her gaze returned to the guard. "My son just sneezed, is what happened. He was joking—not funny to you, I realize."

The woman apparently was not satisfied. "Can I see proof of vaccination and citizenship, please?"

Sloan handed her their documents. "Joel had a negative COVID test recently." She thrust his paperwork in the woman's direction.

"You said he sneezed. I'm going to ask you to pull over for a temperature check. Please proceed that way. Follow the signs to the building." The guard's expression brooked no argument.

With a sigh, Sloan pulled out of line and headed to the low-slung, bland but official-looking building.

After the digital thermometer hovered over Joel's forehead and hers, their documents were reviewed and scanned, then the barrage of questions began. "Any fever? Vomiting? Coughing? Diarrhea? Shortness of breath? Any COVID?"

Then and only then did the officers direct Sloane to return to her car.

Sloane bit her lip as Joel deflated and sank back in his seat. *At least he talked.* One tantrum had caused enough trouble, she could only hope there wouldn't be more.

Joel raised his stuffed animal to the old pacifier strung around Mr. Ted E. Bear's collar. Sloane groaned inside. Joel had resurrected the comfort bear due to the stress of — *Don't go there. Focus on the positive.*

After an hour or so of driving in silence, Sloane glanced in the rearview mirror. Her precious son, tired from the early morning commute and his outburst, had fallen asleep. She took a deep breath and continued the long drive ahead.

The drive through Canada was long, flat, agricultural, and boring, giving her too much time to think. Her SUV had a GPS to guide her, so she didn't have to fuss with maps. Unfortunately, she did have trouble keeping the memories of the previous months at bay.

Those months were more than a mere nightmare. They were real . . . their new normal. At the time, Sloane thought she had survived the worse when Whitt, her spouse of nearly a decade . . . *Stop. Just stop thinking.* How wrong she had been. That event was merely the beginning.

Despite her strict, self-inflicted admonitions to not think about it, the sordid mishmash of the preceding weeks rose in all its horror. The final straw came when the full weight of Whitt's business ventures reached the news outlets.

Sloane couldn't believe her eyes when she turned onto their quiet, tree-lined street to find it filled with loud TV reporters. The road to her house hosted a hoard of cameras, crews, and newscasters. She had to slam on the brakes when her car was surrounded, everyone clamoring for an interview or comments. Despite having her window rolled up, she heard their rapid-fired, unending questions that she couldn't even answer.

"Did you know? "

"What do you say to the allegations?"

"He bilked hundreds of retirees out of their retirement funds, correct?"

"Were you part of the scheme?

"Is it true he capitalized on the opioid crisis with Big Pharma?"

Sloane didn't see how any of them could hear her if she did answer, not over the racket they made.

"How do you feel now that your husband cost million-dollar losses for so many investors?"

Sloane looked at them as if they were crazy, then rolled down her window and yelled, "How the hell do you think I feel? What a stupid question. Is that the best you can do? This is investigative journalism? I'm angry. Sick. Disgusted. Betrayed. I don't know what the hell he did, why, or anything else. Be sure to tell me when you find out. Deal?"

For a second, the din died down. The reporters just stood there in silence, apparently stunned to get a response.

She took advantage of it. "Back off, damn it."

Sloane revved the engine in warning, then inched her car forward. When she reached her driveway, she drove into the attached garage, closing it behind her.

Recently, Sloane had received documents informing her of Whitt's involvement with investors and investments she knew nothing about. *Who was the man I married? Did he knowingly deceive these people? For his own profit?* Whitt never went into detail about his work. *How could he? What a mess he's left!* The package had included investor threats, letters from the IRS, and something from the Federal Reserve and the frickin' Securities and Exchange Commission! *Lord have mercy! What the hell.*

Sloane had controlled her paycheck, but beyond that, finances were Whitt's area of expertise. *I should have paid attention.* Her fury struck like lightning. *Damn it, no! Whitt was the one who the shouldas applied to. He had no business putting me in this mess. And what about Joel? Did Whitt ever stop to think of him? Sloane Anne Wentworth, you do not have the luxury of being pissed. Get your act together, dammit.* Her sudden growl made Joel stir, but he thankfully didn't wake.

After Whitt's death, Sloane found she had little more than her house, a car, and what was left of her parent's life insurance. Fortunately, she had put that money into an IRA savings account. She continued working in Grosse Pointe Park at *On the Hill,* a prestigious art gallery under *thee* Adrián Ford. However, not long after the funeral, Adrián made it clear Sloane's position was over.

Adrián was polite and professionally cool like always. "My business has taken a hit since all this happened. I'm afraid you're a, well, to be frank, a liability." She handed Sloane a long, ivory, heavy-stock On the Hill envelope. "Here's what I owe you. I'll continue to sell your inventory, but that's all I can do for now. Perverse as it may sound, your work may become, shall we say, more saleable. Temporarily anyway. But I don't think the trend will continue. Unless you want to take it with you? I don't recommend that. However, perhaps later . . ."

Aghast, Sloane choked and shook her head. "Send any proceeds to Bradford Sail Inn, Cape Cod, Massachusetts."

Adrián's brow raised. "I'm sorry, dear. A new start for you, perhaps?"

Sloane bowed her head, took the envelope, and left for home.

Although angry with Whitt, with life, and with herself, she would do as she promised Whitt. It was the last thing he asked of her. *I made a deathbed promise.* So, here she was, heading to Cape Cod via Canada. At least she wasn't back in that black hole where she had gone fetal, so grief-stricken and confused she couldn't face the loss. Coping with Whitt's death was enough, but dealing with the incessant calls from his clients took her into uncharted waters well beyond her depth. Little did the investors know, *she* was treading water herself. The responsibilities laid at her door threatened each day to sink her ship.

Sloane despised the directions her thoughts led her. However, the flat, seemingly endless terrain did nothing to distract them as they spun through her head like the windmills lining the roadside fields.

She gritted her teeth and swallowed her anger. To add insult to injury, Whitt's actions also put her and their child at risk. *Sometimes he didn't give one whit about anyone other than himself.*

Sloane glanced at the fuel gauge, glad to find she had well over half a tank.

Sloane recalled the call informing her that Wittman William Wentworth had succumbed to COVID. She heard someone saying more before the awful call ended, but what was the use of listening? What could they tell her that she didn't know already? Her life went from tootsie rolls to tragedy in ten minutes. One minute she was a soccer mom, the next a single mother.

She now feared losing her son to soul-sucking silence. All because of Whitt. It was all over. Whitt was dead, and her job was gone, she couldn't lose her son as well. She couldn't lose herself either. *Who am I now? What am I gonna do? How do I go on?* She felt like she was clinging to the main drain of life's swimming pool with very short fingernails.

She shook herself mentally and wrenched her thoughts to the present. Didn't her faith teach her that today had enough worries? She didn't need to go back in time or into tomorrow to fret. She had enough on her plate today.

Sloane passed more fields of windmills turning fast in the breeze, creating energy while she tried to find her own momentum to follow through with her promise to Whitt. She could hear his voice echoing endlessly in her mind's ear.

Promise me . . . Cape Cod . . . Find Joe.

CHAPTER FIVE: RUN, RUN, RUNAWAY

In the end, those news reporters and social media trolls drove Sloane out of their home and on her way to Bradford Sail Inn on the coast of Cape Cod Bay. The very same Inn Whitt had spent the best summers of his life with his friend Joe.

Whitt had always promised to take her and that she'd love Cape Cod. "Someday, we'll go there. You'll see what I mean. You'll love it."

Sloane replayed a variation of that frequent mental tape. Its theme was the refrain of the shared dream that peppered their conversations. He always got excited about taking his family to join the Islanders in his idea of paradise.

"The air's refreshing," he'd said as recently as a few months ago. "The sea winds always blowing. Cross-air ventilation through the cottages, it's heaven on earth!

"Let's do it."

But something new had entered Whitt's tone the last time he said it. He seemed serious and sincere, like he would *really* make it happen this time.

Thinking back, I'd asked him outright. "How about this summer?"

But then he'd hedged, adding a caveat. "As soon as I take care of things here. Maybe I can do my work remotely. Everything's done through *Zoom* nowadays. Not sure how good the island's *Wi-Fi* is, but we'll do it. Coronavirus can't last forever, and the border's gonna reopen sooner or later. I promise we'll go. Can you picture it? Sloane's Sail On In Galleria? I have a plan. It'll be my next venture."

Sloane remembered thinking, *Really? I prefer Sloane's Sea She-Shed.* She'd giggled. *I dare anyone to say that five times.*

Sloane had made a name for herself in the Michigan Art world, painting its skies, sunrises, and sunsets with blazing acrylics. She had a knack for capturing the red flames and hot oranges, shading with gold, turquoise, mauve, and peach hues for the best effect. But dare she tackle a seascape? That scared her.

Her paintings were often displayed at *On the Hill*, but it wasn't *her* gallery. She had always dreamed of creating her art in her own studio and selling it in her own gallery. As it stood, she would work several hours a day, then go home to paint, care for their child, rinse, and repeat. She hated Adrián's rigid rules and chaffed under the arrogance and downright entitlement that *On the Hill* represented and encouraged.

Not that she was of the suffering artist stock, but she harbored that compelling hunger, ambition, and desire to strike out on her own, but she couldn't . . . not anymore. Oh, she still had the name, the Grosse Pointe look, the panache, and personal poise, but now her contacts were gone. Thanks to Whitt. Anger reared its head and flared. *I'm so fuckin' pissed. How dare he do this to me? To Joel?*

Whitt had apparently persuaded many of her *On the Hill* clientele to join his business venture—his monkey business. His sins cost her. Fury flew through her system like lightning. *Okay, girlfriend, this is the last time I let this shit bother me.*

Whitt's confident voice resonated through her brain once again with yet another of his promises. "I tell you, Sloane, you won't believe the sea. You must see it for yourself . . . experience it. You'll bring its magic to hundreds of landlocked families who want to take a piece of paradise back home with them. The color, the light, the beauty. Just you wait. I promise we'll go as soon as I land this next venture. No more working for someone else. Your own place's waiting for you."

Yeah right. If only. Whitt always had another venture, then another. Granted, it provided them a lifestyle they enjoyed. Living in Grosse Pointe Park was a good place and an excellent source of inspiration. Lake St. Clair featured brilliant skies — once the gray gave way. Her pallet was perpetually in use. Michigan sunsets were rivaled only by those in Hawaii in their magnificence. Even Michigan's gray skies took on a pearly opulence few could fully appreciate but could find in her paintings.

People often walked away feeling better after viewing her renderings of gray skies, seeing the often-felt dreary day in a whole new light — bearable and less oppressive. Her paintings gave them a new appreciation of the drab cloudy atmosphere by making the moody skies shimmer and glow. The fact that she lived on the lake gave her plenty of opportunities to capture the sky's many moods. She always kept her sketch pad and phone nearby so she could use them when time permitted, and her muse was hot.

With an effort, Sloane shook her moody feelings off.

CHAPTER SIX: THERE'S A PLACE

Sloane was relieved Joel napped. A lot had happened recently, and she had literally found next to no time to process it all. Her psyche demanded its due now, and to get through the jumble of her life, she had to face her fears head-on, no matter how hard she tried to banish them. Her issues wouldn't vanish on their own. *Geesh, which crisis do I face first? Whitt's death or his crimes? Our future or my past? Whitt? Investment Fraud? Widowhood? Is widowhood even a word, a thing, a condition of life? How could Whitt up and die on me, leaving such a mess behind? What the hell.*

Addie, her old college roommate, had completed her degree in social work when tragedy called Sloane back home in 2011. Addie had been her rock then and now functioned as her armchair therapist. Addie sagely advised Sloane to embrace her demons. She just wasn't sure how or in what order. Her dad often told her when you don't know what to do, do what comes *next to do*. So, she did just that. She took her next step by facing her *immediate* scary future. Get to Cape Cod and find Joe, as promised. Sometimes, having your old college roommate as an unofficial therapist and a dad with corny, simple advice wasn't all that helpful. Other times, it came in handy.

Sloane despised the directions her thoughts led her, but the endless terrain apparently allowed her psyche to tumble through memories like sun-dried leaves in the autumn breeze. *Just let it happen. This is the therapy Addie suggested, remember?*

40

She gritted her teeth, cried, and tried to carry on, to face her fears, and move forward. But the tears blurred her vision and made her nose run, proving the impossibility of the task. Thoughts of recent events seemed overwhelming. Was she grieving? Was she stuck in the anger part of grief? *How can I ever accept what he's done to us? How dare he?*

She glanced at the fuel gauge, which indicated a need to stop at the next rest plaza.

Sloane woke Joel playfully, poking his shoulder and helping him free himself from the booster seat. "You slept through the first part of a foreign country. What kind of an explorer are you?"

Joel giggled. She was pleased to hear that sound again after far too long. Not since Whitt's death . . . A new light glimmered in Joel's eyes that had been dimmed, and a smile replaced his usual sadness.

"So how do you like Canada so far, sleepyhead?"

"Boring."

Sloane smiled. "The best is yet to come. Niagara Falls! Let's use the restroom and get some lunch. How about Mickey D's?" An unaccustomed treat, a rarity, really.

Joel responded with a spirited fist pump and an unexpected, "Yes!"

Overjoyed, Sloane ordered her son a burger, fries, pop, and an apple pie instead of a *Happy Meal*. It wasn't her typical anti-junk food choice, but she was celebrating the fact he used words, not his usual grunts and gestures.

Joel's eyes popped when he saw his feast. He tore into it, probably fearing she would change her mind.

Sloane hoped this trip, with the ocean at the end and natural wonders along the way, would reawaken Joel's desire to talk and help to end his silence and sadness. Joel's therapist said he most likely suffered temporary selective mutism due to the trauma of his father's sudden death and the onslaught of the reporters. The hounding got so intense that they stayed with Addie—still another transition for Joel—until the news cycle ended. When it stopped, she packed their bags and made a reservation for Bradford Sail Inn on Cape Cod. Whitt had at least left her with a place to run to.

They drove on, and this time Joel kept an eye open, looking for Niagara Falls. While her GPS may be a great feature, following it proved challenging. She often didn't hear directions for the correct lane early enough, and the signs along the highway were easily passed before she could react to them. As a result, she missed the exit that would have taken them to the Canadian side of the falls. Instead, she exited and found herself navigating the American side. To top it off, she discovered two cities named Niagara Falls—one in Canada and the other in America.

It didn't help when they *saw* the mist created by the falls from their car windows but couldn't get *to* the falls. She got trapped on the American side and lost in Niagara Falls State Park. When it started raining, Sloane let loose a heavy sigh. "Leave it to us to *miss* one of the eight wonders of the world. Takes a whole new level of ridiculous to achieve that." *Damn it.* After turning in the opposite direction, she freed them from the unending trap of navigating Niagara Falls State Park.

She took the first turnoff that led to a four-lane—in each direction—highway. *What a disaster of a side trip.* She had just begun to calm down when Joel started fussing about needing a bathroom.

"What do you mean? We just stopped at that rest stop in the park, and you said you didn't have to go!" she snapped.

Joel responded by kicking the back of her seat repeatedly and howling at the top of his lungs, "Gotta peeeee!"

Sloane began to sweat, and her nerves were shot. She made a quick left turn—illegally crossing four lanes—into a gas station only to find it abandoned and locked.

Joel howled, shattering what was left of her control.

She slammed the car into park and pointed. "Pee in those bushes behind the gas station."

"Nooooo!"

"Just do it. There's nowhere else to go."

Forced by necessity, he complied, still crying. Sloane hustled him back into the car and pulled onto the highway, only to find she was headed toward Toronto. Her GPS squawked, *Recalculating. Make a U-turn.* She couldn't do that. It simply wasn't possible.

Suddenly, Joel yelled. "I'm not buckled!"

She panicked. "Damn it to Hell! Buckle up."

"C-C-Can't."

What kind of mother leaves her kid not properly seat belted? She was in the middle of the frickin' highway but quickly spotted a place to pull onto the shoulder. She got out of the car and opened the side door. When she had him buckled in, she sank against the car, breathing hard. Once back in the driver's seat, she googled the nearest motel. *Eff our reservation in Liverpool. We're stopping here.*

It didn't matter to her if the motel was a one-star or a five-star. If it had the basics and was clean, she was good. The closest place was a 1950s-style motel called Night's Inn for two hundred bucks. When she remarked on the price, the skinny kid at the counter, wearing low-slung baggie pants, gave her a funny look.

He shrugged. "Niagara Falls pricing, lady. You want it or not?"

Sloane handed him her credit card and pulled out her driver's license. Mercifully, they found a diner within walking distance that served coney dogs. Her hands shook as she ate her hotdog, wishing she had a *Xanax.* Or wine. Or a beer. Or something stronger like a Manhattan. Hungry and worn out by the entire day, Joel finally calmed down and retreated into his silent mode. When they returned to their room, they put their PJs on and fell asleep watching *The Masked Singer,* sharing the king-sized bed.

Sloane awoke to the early morning cartoon that Joel was watching. She took a quick shower and put on some clothes, then googled their whereabouts to get them back on track while Joel got himself cleaned and dressed. The directions indicated they needed to drive the New York Thruway, which became the Massachusetts Turnpike at the boundary between the states.

She programmed the car, promising Joel breakfast at the first service plaza. "We've got a full-day drive ahead of us. What DVD do you want to watch?"

Joel rifled through the assortment and selected *Wall-E* and *The Muppets Take Manhattan.* He giggled when she told him Manhattan was in New York, and they were in New York, too.

True to her word, they grabbed breakfast sandwiches and orange juice when she refueled. Joel didn't balk this time when she suggested he use the restroom—just in case. They drove for several hours. It didn't take long before the scenery began to change.

"Put the movie on pause a moment, Joel. Look out the window. See those hills out there? Pretty soon, we'll climb higher, and we'll be skirting the Adirondack mountains. Now we're in the foothills."

"Where are the toes? Are we tickling them now as we drive through?"

Sloane chuckled. "Good one, son. Ha, ha."

"Do you think the feet wear socks?" His tone was jovial . . . playful. "Get it?"

"Hardee har har. Yes, stinky mossy ones."

Soon, she heard the movie soundtrack again and knew his attention was back on the Muppets. She meant to expand on the geography and topography lesson but chose to do it another time. *Take the win, Sloane. He's talking more. Do jokes count? Duh. Doesn't take a degree in rocket science to figure that out. Of course, it counts.*

Sloane had to have faith in Joel's therapist's claim that, sooner or later, Joel would snap out of his mutism. *Perhaps this trip to the ocean will help him get better. Give him something to talk about. What matters right now is Joel seems happier and is joking. I haven't heard any eight-year-old jokes since Whitt died. Maybe my son is already getting better. Is that too much to ask?* She could only hope.

Sloane also prayed her anger at Whitt would pass away like he had. *It sucks to be mad at a dead man, but I am so frickin' furious with him I could spit . . . no, make that shit fire and cremate him all over again.*

Back in college, Sloane had left the embarrassing traumatic experience she'd suffered in Ann Arbor in her past when she had to rush home to help her mother. She managed to find time to finish her degree in Fine Arts at Wayne State University, where she had met Whitt.

Sloane had also joined the Sky Club at WSU to finish her flight lessons for her pilot's license. Thankfully, she retained credit for what flying she had completed with he-whose-name-will-never-be-spoken. *Some Superman he was. Thank God I met Whitt.*

Whitt had become much more than a handsome distraction when her mom's care required rehabilitation, nursing home care, and ultimately hospice care. *How did I ever live through all that?* But she knew what the answer was—Whitt, her art, and flying. *I love slipping the bonds of Earth and soaring on silvered wings.* She had claimed John Gillespie Magee Jr's poem, *High Flight*, as her private pilot's prayer as well as her go-to poem.

She smiled. She was now free to soar above her grief, her anger, her fear. Although, she currently had no idea how she could survive, care for Joel, or create a new life for them. She had a degree but no real marketable skills. Legally, things at home were a mess, but she wasn't going to think of that now. Whitt had begged her to find Joe in Cape Cod, which she *could* do. *Will I make it? Can I? Do I have a choice? No, I do not, but I will survive. How well is the question.*

CHAPTER SEVEN: I WILL SURVIVE

Sloane stopped at a service plaza just after crossing into Massachusetts. She once again broke her fast-food rule when Joel asked for a lobster roll—at *McDonald's*, of all places.

"Daddy loved lobster rolls, too." A cloud passed over Joel's face when she mentioned his father, but he quickly recovered. "Sick." Which in Joel-speak meant *good*.

They spent the better part of the day driving through the state and ran into the tourist traffic, alerting her that the last fifty miles would be slow. She noticed license plates from all over the east coast but none from Michigan. She had learned there were fewer cars and SUVs than the weekend would bring, but enough to cause a slowdown and backup at Bourne Bridge, one of the two bridges linking the mainland to Cape Cod. She was glad she'd packed her patience and didn't mind that Joel was watching *YouTube*.

She was about to resume her mom-alogue to draw his attention to the bridge, but surprisingly, he noticed it all by himself.

He yelled. "Wicked bridge. Ocean?"

She hesitated a minute, speaking to herself as much as to him. "They call it the Cape Cod Canal, but the water must be part of the ocean since Cape Cod is an island." *Although technically, it's a peninsula with a canal in between.* She focused on the traffic and the mazelike roads she was driving. "Keep an eye out for whales."

It took almost as long to cross this bridge as the slow trudge they had experienced across the Blue Water Bridge in

Michigan. When she found herself on the Cape Code side, she breathed a sigh of relief, only to learn she'd have to deal with a rotary ahead. She avoided roundabouts in Michigan, but she really had no choice here. The automated GPS voice told her to turn right at the second exit. She gripped the wheel so tight her knuckles whitened, but she made the loop onto Sandwich Road. She relaxed when they turned onto Route 6 a short time later.

"Where's the beach?"

He's talking . . . asking questions . . . "On the other side of these trees."

"Are you sure?" Joel sounded skeptical. "This looks like home. Same trees."

"I'm sure. See how these trees are twisted and low to the ground? The trade winds—winds from the ocean—blew them over, making them grow crooked."

Joel persisted. "We have those same bushes in our backyard."

"We're on Cape Cod. The ocean is here. Trust me. There're beaches, too."

"Where are the palm trees?"

Sloane held onto her patience, wanting to keep Joel talking, and kept her tone even. "There aren't any here."

His voice started to rise. "You said Daddy lived on an island."

"That's right. He spent his summers here." Then the lightbulb went on in her head. "This isn't a *tropical* island."

Joel got louder. "You said we were going to Daddy's island. Where's the pink hotel?"

"Pink hotel?"

"Yeah. You stayed in the pink hotel. It had palm trees."

Thankfully, she wouldn't have to follow GPS directions for a while, which was hard under normal circumstances, but with Joel's piercing wails, it would be practically impossible.

"We'll talk about it later. Why don't you watch for signs saying Bradford Sail Inn? That's where we're going. There'll be a beach and sand, you'll see."

"I wanna see where you and Daddy had your money moon. On the island."

Money moon? What? Then she understood. *I had forgotten the joke Whitt would make every time our honeymoon came up because it was so expensive in Hawaii. This is not the time to discuss money moons, honeymoons, or anything else.*

Joel repeatedly kicked the back of her seat. She bit her lips so hard that her lower lip started bleeding.

Sloane choked down her frustration. *Lord, please, no tantrum now.* They were getting close to their destination, but it had been a long day already.

Joel was tired.

She was tired.

She didn't need another one of Joel's meltdowns. Not now. Not ever. *Motherhood seriously sucks sometimes.*

"I'll explain later, Joel. Look for Shore Road. That's where we turn left." She prayed giving him a task would distract him, but it didn't do much.

She passed a sign for Wellfleet, hoping they were supposed to. Bradford Sail Inn was on Shore Road. She gritted her teeth until she heard the GPS directing, *Turn left onto Shore Road.* She did and was suddenly on a narrow two-lane street fringed with cute cottages with cedar shake roofs.

Sloane came to a rise in the road, where she could see the ocean skirt the sandy beach. The late afternoon sun sparkled on the waves, and a tall monument rose on the far side of the Cape's curve in the distance. It created a postcard-perfect panoramic view. Beautiful. She held her breath as the landscape greeted her like a soulmate, and she knew she had come home. Then the road dipped, and she was level with the beach and the cottages dotting the sand and roadside.

A mile or two later, Joel tugged on her shirt collar and

49

shouted, "There." He pointed to a sign reading *Bradford Sail Inn and Tradewinds*.

Even though the winds weren't technically trade winds as defined, folks in the area referred to them that way. A mountain of blue and purple hydrangeas grew in the space beneath the sign.

Sloane parked in front of a small clapboard one-story cottage labeled *Office* and released the breath she'd been holding with a whoosh. She sank against the wheel, relieved beyond belief. She had never driven this far in her life. *I did it.* She took a deep breath, determined to make a good and solid secure future for herself and her son. She pried Joel loose from the cocoon of blankets, pillows, toys, books, DVDs, and the seatbelt.

She wasn't sure what she expected when she entered the office, but it wasn't a small, cramped space, overrun with papers covering every surface, even the computer keyboard.

Joel had obviously found a small bell on the reception counter. *Ding, ding, ding.* "Hello. Anybody here?"

A big shaggy dog barreled in and jumped onto Joel, placing a paw on each shoulder as if planning to hug him. The beast slobbered drooling kisses on Joel's face. In quick pursuit came a body attached to a flying ponytail belonging to a young girl. She tackled the pooch, who took to licking her, too. Both children were laughing.

"Whaley, stay. Yuck. Stop kissing." Whaley ignored the girl's command and continued washing Joel's face.

Joel joined the free-for-all, rolling around with the dog.

In moments, a slight, older woman, the epitome of a Cape Cod native, came to the girl's aid—albeit a bit wobbly. She grasped Whaley by the collar and led him away. "Down Boy. Sorry 'bout that. He gets excited easily. Janie, you, and your new friend should find the Frisbee and distract Whaley."

Janie whined, "But Whaley needs a bath. I can do it."

A firm tone entered the woman's voice. "Wait for me."

"I bet my mommy'd let me—"

"I'm not your mommy."

"Uncle Joe would understand."

The woman threw her a hard look.

"Fine. Come on, kid. Let's find the Frisbee." The old screen door banged after Janie, Joel, and Whaley trooped outside.

"I'm Monalisa." The woman paused, catching her breath. "Pardon the doggie welcome. I'll just help them and be back in a flash."

Sloane smiled. "No harm done. Joel's not complaining. I haven't seen him smile in a long time."

Monalisa returned, brushing her hands. "There, that's settled. How can I help you?"

"I'm Sloane—"

"We've been expecting you. Even though it's not the weekend, traffic always creates delays. You're in cottage nine B, *Sea Breeze Cottage*. There are four rows of cottages separated by the green grass commons near the hydrangea. They're beautiful this time of year. Enjoy. There's parking next to the sign." Monalisa pushed a real key—not a keycard—in Sloane's direction. "Oh, and we have food trucks come in each evening if you want to grab a quick bite. They set up on the commons from five through seven p.m."

Sloane was pleased. "The beach and a food truck. How did we get so lucky?"

"The beach is plenty deep enough, depending on how much the winter erodes away. Your son will be able to play outside your door without worry. Take the boardwalk to get down to the shoreline. There are wheel carts for luggage if you need help moving in. Housekeepers come every day. You get fresh sheets on Saturdays." Monalisa glanced down at the old ledger. "I see you're paid up for two weeks. If you decide to stay longer, let us know as soon as you possibly can." She winked. "These cottages are booked for weeks in advance, but

51

I usually can squeeze people in. The *Tradewinds* have both ef-ficiencies as well as simple rooms."

Sloane took the key and went on her way. The screen door banged as she left. Her car kicked up gravel as she wound her way through the parking lot. The well-weathered walls of the cottages were whitewashed with black roofs and shutters. It looked like something you'd expect to find in New England's rich colonial past.

Sloane passed several similar cottages and kept an eye out for 9B. Ahead she could see the ocean still sparkling in the late afternoon sun. The waves seem to snatch the sunlight, making the water look like rolling liquid gold. The view was spectac-ular.

The breezy air, cooled by the steady trade winds, would make their lugging, tugging, and moving in more comforta-ble. The sea air held the right amount of brine that Sloane breathed it in eagerly.

Joel seemed to relish pushing the cart holding their belong-ings and did a good job keeping it on the narrow sidewalk. It would probably take at least two trips to get everything into the cottage. She was glad she had followed advice to pack ex-tra items such as beach paraphernalia, a coffeemaker, and food staples. The breakfast items would come in handy be-cause she was too drained to grocery shop after the long trip.

Sloane was delighted to see picnic tables conveniently placed outside each unit, affording an opportunity to eat while enjoying the view of the ocean. *Aha, there it is . . . nine-B.* She unlocked the door and entered. Joel jumped up the small stoop leading to the door and hopped in behind her.

The décor reflected a 1950s retro cottage. The open concept showcased a small well-equipped kitchen, a living room with a comfy-looking daybed and a decent flatscreen TV, and a small dining area with a round maple table surrounded by four vintage barrel-back chairs. The bedroom was a good size with two double-size maple beds, a nightstand between them, a large dresser, and an ample closet with louvered doors. A small but updated bathroom with an old-fashioned tub and shower completed the cottage floorplan.

When she tested the mattress on one of the beds, she found herself in heaven. From the bed, she could look out at Cape Cod Bay and see the calm ocean with its gentle waves. She fell in love with the cottage and its charm. It was the most delightful place she had ever seen—perfect in its rustic simplicity.

The sea winds blew through the open windows, and the curtains billowed gently in the breeze. The screen door locked using a simple hook that rattled in its fixings when used. The salt air had slightly warped the door, causing it to bang shut each time they went through it, which only added to her delight.

While Sloane got everything unpacked and put away, Joel cartwheeled through the living room, helping a little. Her boy never walked when he could run, skip, jump, or hop.

The sun was about to set by the time she finished getting them settled. "I'm hungry as a whale. Wanna check out that food truck?"

Sloane and Joel walked back to the parking lot following the greenway—a long slash of grass the brochure called *The Green*—where they found *Chicks by the Sea* food truck. Sloane treated herself to clam chowder and a lobster roll. Joel selected clam strips and sweet potato fries, which she felt made up for the fast-food fare her son had been eating on the trip.

They carried the food back to the cottage and sat at their picnic table watching the corals, reds, and purples of the sunset stain both sea and sky. Solar lights lit the boardwalk that led to the beach and continued along the dock to a small marina. She loved hearing the waves slap against the hulls of the various boats tied there.

Folks lined the boardwalk to chase the sunset, which

rivaled Michigan's. As darkness fell, Sloan was too tired to launch into a mom-alogue. She was surprised by the display of the Milky Way. She couldn't remember the last time she had even seen them. The bright city lights at home eclipsed them. She nearly forgot they existed! Joni Mitchel was right when she sang about not knowing what ya got till it's gone.

The night was warm, and the windows were wide open already, so Sloane didn't close the shades since the breeze would only make them slap in and out all night long. The lengthy drive, the fresh sea air, plus the sound of the surf sang a lullaby that put hers to shame. Although there were two beds, Joel crawled into hers and burrowed next to her. Knowing moments like this wouldn't last forever and would be abandoned someday sooner than she'd like, she allowed them both the snuggly comfort.

The following morning, Sloane was glad she had packed the coffeemaker. The cottage offered an old stove-top percolator, which she had no idea how to use. She supposed she could google how, but why? Her *Keurig* would do just fine.

Sloane wasn't sure how well the *Wi-Fi* connection was or if the Inn was even connected. When they had passed a library coming in, she found people sitting on the steps with their devices, perhaps hoping to pick up a signal. She wasn't awake enough to do a search anyway.

A few seconds later, she had her brew in hand and opened the cottage door to a beautiful summer blue sky. A lone but strikingly white, feathery cloud stretched across the endless expanse. The beach grasses nearby waved in the breeze. She smiled, already in love with the sea winds lending a slight nip to the air, making her glad she wore flannel PJs. When she looked toward the beach, the ocean greeted her like a best friend.

She stepped outside and pulled up one of the two white

plastic chairs. She stretched her legs before her and warmed her face with the rising steam from her favorite hazelnut blend. She was in heaven, experiencing for herself why Whitt liked it here so much. For the first time in forever, her heart lifted.

It was early, and Joel was still sleeping, so she let herself enjoy the setting. One by one, other people drifted outside to greet the morning, too. Like her, they had steaming mugs in their hands. Many of the guests also wore their thermal PJs or robes to greet the day. Cape Cod just seemed like the kind of place where you wanted to get *out there.* Become one with the sea, the sky.

Sloane felt the call to soar like the seagulls cawing in the breeze. The first of the sun's rays reached the sand as if to wake it up. The early risers were quiet as if this time was sacred and not to be disturbed while children still slept.

The bleary-eyed, newly awake smiled a nod to each other as they made their way to picnic tables or chairs. No one carried a book, a device, or a newspaper. The view and peace of the moment beat any church or cathedral she had ever been inside. Gradually, tousled kids woke up, rubbing their eyes as they joined their bed-headed parents in what appeared to be a morning ritual. All eyes turned to the east as the sea and sky said hello, promising a great day with a spectacular sunrise.

Sloane felt a calm wash over her that she'd never be capable of putting into words. She wanted to weep. Not in pain this time, but for the perfect blend of elements—sun, white clouds, sky, water, wind, surf, salt.

Joel came outside and said it all in one word. "Awesome."

Sloane ruffled his hair and decided to make pancakes, glad she brought the basics with her. Thankfully, she needed only water, no eggs or milk. *God bless whoever invented this mix.* They ate breakfast outside, facing the sea, then dressed for the day. Afterward, they took the boardwalk down to the shore-line, picking up shells and whatnot. Sand toys were strewn along the way, the sun rose higher in the sky, and life at the Bradford Sail Inn got busy. Folks started packing totes, beach chairs, multi-color sun umbrellas, and coolers, then spread out on the beach. Others flew kites in the trade winds while some families made their way to the pool.

Sloan needed to do what came next, and the most immediate *next* was groceries and finding Joe Bradford. She decided to kill two birds with one stone. She held Joel's hand as they walked through the cottage community to return to the office. Janie and Whaley were apparently otherwise occupied, and a different young gal was at the reception desk.

She smiled at the girl. "Hello. I'm looking for two things. A grocery store and Joe Bradford."

The girl smiled back. "Fortunately, I can help. Follow Shore Road toward the sea and turn left to find the *market*. You can find Joe at the Wing It kiosk on the pier off Commercial Street in Provincetown. You can't miss him. Handsome hunk, wearing a baseball cap. Tall. Built." She winked. "You single? You could do worse. He's the whole thing." The gal winked again. "And a lot of a good guy."

Sloane snorted. "As if. I'm not looking for trouble."

"Anything else I can help you with?"

Sloane smiled. "Got any winning lottery tickets?"

The twenty-something girl laughed. "No such luck, but you can buy some in P-town."

"P-town?"

"Provincetown. Tourists and locals shorten it to P-town."

Joel giggled. "Hope they have a lot of bathrooms. Get it, Mom? Pee town."

Sloane groaned, but she was happy that at least her jokester spoke.

They left and walked to her SUV, passing a charming arbor

of wisteria. Next to it were the brilliant blue, white, and purple hydrangea bushes. They were the healthiest hydrangea she had ever seen. The salt air and sunshine must account for the pretty profusion.

It was much easier buckling Joel into the booster seat since there were no cumbersome pillows, teddy bears, and blankets to contend with.

She decided to let the breeze blow her the way she should go. However, tempting glimpses of water caught beyond cottage gardens and beaches lured her closer and closer to the MacMillan Pier, not the grocery mart. She parked in a lot alongside the pier, paying an exorbitant fee, then spotted the bus terminus and decided to check into that for next time.

The sea was serene, dotted with parasailers in the distance. The white canvas sails of sailboats also traversed Cape Cod Bay, providing a bright contrast to the sea and sky. She sucked in a breath at the beauty of the seascape that filled her with something close to joy . . . most importantly, hope.

The long boardwalk of the pier beckoned. The day was pleasant, the sun warm and comfortable, but not hot. Along the way, photo ops were available where Joel could put his face in a cutout to become a sea captain on a ship or a merman. He preferred the pirate with a peg leg and parrot.

The many kiosks spaced here and there along the walk offered sea glass jewelry, artwork, or knick-knacks with an ocean or nautical theme. Part of the pier contained docks for fishing boats, whale-watching crafts, and other boats. A fishing charter was preparing its catch and throwing pieces to the nearby seals.

Joel was beside himself and started chattering about the sharks and seals. "What if a shark gets the seal? I read they eat them. Do you think it will?" He peppered her with questions, and she celebrated each one.

They strolled the boardwalk, savoring the sights and

smells, snapping photos every so often.

Joel read a sign outside a larger building. "It's a Pirate Museum, Mom! Can we go, can we?"

She laughed. "Yes, but not today. We have some stuff to do — like grocery shopping, remember?"

"Ain't no supermarket here, Mom."

"Look for Wing It. I have someone to see there."

Distracted by the task, Joel fashioned a spyglass with his hands and peered around. "There she blows. I found it." He pointed, then thankfully busied himself watching the water through his handmade telescope.

And indeed, Joel had spied the kiosk for Wing It. The beach shack with an old-fashioned biplane must have drawn Joel's eye like a beacon. According to the brochure she picked up from the counter, *Wing It* offered tourist sightseeing flights and whale-watching from the sky.

A tall, well-built man in a t-shirt wearing a baseball cap and cargo shorts was busy talking to prospective customers. Sloane could not clearly see the guy's face because the family crowded the counter. From what she overheard, the group was booking an excursion. When they walked away, the man turned his back to her, presumably entering the data into the computer. It was clear he had not seen them.

She cleared her throat to capture his attention. "Excuse me, I'm looking for Joe."

The man turned around with a smile. "Looks like you found him."

Sloane froze. "Fancy meeting you here," she replied.

"Seth?"

"Sloane? What on earth are you doing here?"

Chapter Eight: I've Been Everywhere

Sloane could only stare at the man she thought she would never see again. Seth didn't move a muscle either, but his eyes widened. Confusion and something else crossed his sun-kissed face, and a week's worth of stubble dusted his cheeks.

He tilted his head. "I hate to repeat myself, but what are you doing here?"

Sloane shot right back. "I could ask you the same question."

Seth squinted. "Seriously, Sloane. It is *you*, right?"

She nodded. "Sloane Wentworth at your service. And to answer your question, I'm looking for Joe Bradford."

His hands swept out to the side as he made a half bow. "Here he is. I'm your man."

It was Sloane's turn to be confused. "What?"

"Joe is standing right in front of you."

She felt an ice-cold ripple slither down her spine despite the warm summer sun on her skin. "What are you, a stand-up comedian now? You're Seth."

"Yeah . . . so I am. Seth *Joseph* Bradford, otherwise known locally as *Joe*, Joe Bradford. My Pops was the original Seth, so they called me by my middle name to tell us apart. What can I do for you?"

Sloane huffed. "You tell me."

"How would I know?"

At that moment, Sloane wished she wore bangs so her huff of frustration would carry some punch. "This isn't funny, Seth, *Joe*, whoever the hell you are. I'm Wittman Wentworth's

59

widow."

Concern crossed his face. "Whitt? Whitt's wife?"

She suddenly choked up. "Whitt's widow." Unbidden tears welled in her eyes, threatening to spill.

Seth's hand shot out, touching hers. "Oh my God, Sloane, I'm so sorry."

Heat ran through her from his touch. She pulled her hand away and cleared her throat. Impatient with her show of emotion, she flicked the gathering moisture away from her eyes before it could form those dreaded too-ready tears.

Seth clearly noticed but didn't comment on them. "Whitt was my best friend."

Sloane took a deep breath to calm down. In control of herself again, she straightened. "Really? Hmm. That must be why you were chosen to be the best man at our wedding. Oh, wait a minute, you weren't, were you? Ever heard the term *RSVP*? Oh, it's coming back to me now. No, you did not. In fact, you didn't even show up for the wedding. At all. Not that I even knew you were, well, *you*." She shook her head, mad at herself for letting him unnerve her, making her insides quiver.

"Sorry 'bout that, Sloane. I was out of the country. Seems like Whitt didn't tell you—"

"Turns out there's a lot Whitt didn't tell me."

Seth windmilled his arms. "Hell, man, I've been everywhere. I enlisted in the Air Force after nine-eleven. My work was classified."

"As I said, there's so much I don't know. Like why did Whitt—on his death bed no less—tell me to find *Joe*? Surely, you've read the newspapers, heard the news, the debacle, the scandal?"

Seth-slash-Joe slapped a hand to his forehead. "Oh, good God. I didn't realize you . . . you were . . . involved."

Sloane drew herself up. "I was *not*, thank you very much."

60

Seth's face got red. "I didn't mean that. Of course, you weren't. I'm an idiot. In shock at seeing you again and here." He winked and shook his head. "Of all the gin joints . . . I'm surprised, at the very least. I'm sorry, but I thought he married someone named Lonnie."

Sloane sighed. "He called me that. Said I didn't look like a Sloane."

He smiled with a twinkle in his eyes. "Hmm, Sloane is a good fit for a classy broad like you."

Joel bopped to her side and pulled on her arm. "Mooom . . ." He tried dragging her away from the kiosk, clearly wanting to let her know he was ready to go.

Seth dropped to his knee in front of Joel, gaining the boy's attention. "Yo-ho there, matey, I'm *Joe* to folks around here, but to your mom, I'm Seth." Seth winked. "Are you ready to fly?"

Joel's face lit with excitement. "For reals?"

Seth nodded and stood. "How 'bout it, *Mooom*? You wanna get high?"

"Said the spider to the fly." Sloane winced at her automatic response. "I think we've already covered that ground."

"Afraid, eh?"

Sloane snorted. "Hardly." She sniffed. "As if."

"I've heard that before."

Joel bounced up and down like a bobber in the wind-tossed waves. "Mom flies airplanes, too. But she doesn't take me very much. Can we go, Mom? Can we?" His puppy-dog eyes were hard to resist.

Seth spoke up. "Hold on there, cowboy. Flying here isn't easy. For starters, the wind is fierce. The runway — if you can call it that — is a narrow strip. Then there's sand dunes, and there's the water on three sides to contend with. Best you go up with an experienced pilot, like me." He thumped his chest with his thumb.

Sloane sent him a hard look. "I am experienced." When she heard her own words, she flushed. "Pilot . . . I'm an experienced pilot."

Seth didn't quite manage to hide his grin.

She continued. "Did you think I wouldn't follow through and get my credentials? I have my license. I can deal. I just need a bird."

Speculation shone in Seth's gaze. "Why would I think a girl like you would quit? Au contraire, my dear. You always did have spunk—"

"Skill, you mean." She interrupted. "Not spunk. I have skill."

His brow quirked. "As a matter of fact, I have several planes at my disposal. I'm always looking for a pilot. I could put you to work—once you learned the ropes, that is."

"Don't tell me you're suggesting I learn them from you."

He grinned. "Okay, I won't. But I can still take you up and show you the island. Give you some suggestions for where to go and what to do while you're on Cape Cod. Maybe you could even help me out by flying for Wing It. Like I said, I'm always looking."

She groaned. *More like looking for trouble. Is he flirting with me?*

Chapter Nine: Show Me the Way

Sloane shook herself. She was chagrined by her reaction to the skin-to-skin contact when Seth had touched her arm in sympathy, but she still had to stop at the P-town grocer's. She made her goodbyes, promising to talk later.

She spied a nearby *clam* shack and decided to grab lunch before they stopped at the grocery store. Joel ordered *chicken* — of all things, *Kids* — she smiled and threw up her hands at the irony. She had learned it was better to shop on a full stomach, having found herself falling into the empty stomach trap way too often, buying too much and paying the price. She'd bet her last dime that prices on the island would already be sky-high due to inflation.

As Sloane and Joel walked back to the parking lot, she enjoyed the sights and sounds of their surroundings, from the raucous caw of the various sea birds to the musical laughter of the tourists. She recognized the black cormorants but didn't know the others. The ever-vigilant gulls hovered around the pier, snagging food wherever they could from tourists, waste bins, and fishermen preparing their catch for sale.

A hoard of hawkers plied people with brochures advertising tours, trips, and activities. Joel accepted every pamphlet offered, making her chuckle. It'd be fun to see what was available on the island. *Might as well explore the place while we're here.*

She saw a bus with a flashing digital LED bar across the top, offering a two-dollar fare to the National Seashore Museum, and made a note to check that out. After all, the bus fare was way cheaper than parking, and her financial future was

63

far from secure.

Money was another issue to figure out. Sloane couldn't do that on a sidewalk near the pier. She fought valiantly to put the matter out of her mind and stay in the moment like all the self-help books suggested.

She found her car and used the fob to unlock the doors. Once inside the car, she opened the windows and the sunroof to take advantage of the sea winds. *I love these winds. Loved 'em in Hawaii, love 'em here.* Her emotional and physical thermostats ran hot, so the breeze was a gift, one of life's little treasures. She relaxed, going with the flow as she headed to the grocery store.

Driving down Commercial Street was torture. Cars, pedestrians, and delivery trucks crowded the narrow street competing for passage. Sloane was a nervous wreck until she got out of the hub of the town, finally making it to the supermarket. She parked in the lot and grabbed Joel's hand despite his protests that he wasn't a baby, but the lot was full of vehicles pulling in and out, making it dangerous. Inside, the market was packed to the gills as well. She wondered if it was this busy all week.

It became apparent that most of the shoppers were probably renting a beachside cottage and had the same idea that Sloane did. Everyone appeared to be in the same repeated circuit due to the supermarket's poorly planned layout. She had to make numerous trips back down aisles, looking for items she had apparently passed previously.

There were traffic jams of shopping carts as people meandered about like sardines trapped in a can. Sloane was constantly crying out *excuse me* and *pardon me* as she slipped between baskets and carts to grab some produce, or what have you. Apparently, everyone was as new to the store's floorplan as she was, resulting in too many bodies crammed in the same area at the same time.

Joel had clearly taken advantage of Sloane's distraction—created by seeing Seth and the shoppers—which became obvious when they got back to the cottage. As she unpacked their cache, she found *Doritos* rather than *Wheat Thins, Lucky Charms* in lieu of *Bran Flakes*, and *Pop Tarts* instead of banana muffins or granola bars. The tic of her cheek betrayed her chagrin . . . with herself, not her son. It was clear Seth got to her. The *Doritos* proved that much. She was simply not paying attention.

The small kitchen prevented Joel from helping, saving him from a lecture on junk food and healthy living. Sloane unpacked while Joel played on the sand outside their cottage. The beach was deep and broad—perfect for young children and their parents because the dangers of the ocean were a long boardwalk away.

She heard voices of multiple families chatting as they passed her cottage, which was at the end of the row. Anyone who wanted to use the beach, walk the boardwalk, or lounge on the beach had to pass her place. Curiosity drew her outside to see what caused the sudden exodus. A small berm blocked her view, but soon she saw children and parents walking onto the wet sand, bending here and there, and talking excitedly about whatever they found. It didn't take long to realize she was seeing her first low tide.

"Come on, Joel, let's see what this is all about." Sloane took his hand as they walked down to the shore, occasionally stopping as they discovered shells, feathers, and other scattered sea bits. Joel was fascinated by the remains of small crustaceans dotting the sand, no doubt cast aside by the hungry sea birds. He looked like he was in seventh heaven each time he found a claw or crab leg remnant, shoving them in his pocket. She made a mental note to find a mason jar to hold his cache.

The receding shoreline revealed an interesting array of detritus left behind, a treasure trove for adults and children alike. Shells, creatures, seaweed, driftwood, and more were just awaiting discovery. An artist could have a field day with the imagery, and amateur ocean life aficionados would be lost to discovery. Cries of delight filled the air, the oos and aahs adding to the ocean's soundscape.

"Just think, Joel, we're walking on the bottom of the sea. Cool huh? Can't find this in our backyard."

Joel looked up from his find, what looked like a clamshell, and smiled. The light in his eyes shone brightly, and with the color in his cheeks, he looked healthy and—dare she say—happy.

"Stop a minute. Look up. Look all around. Take this all in. Listen to the sea. This is the life."

Sloane was smiling, too. For the first time in a long time, she felt good. The wind lifted her hair and blew it away from her face. *Good Lord, for the first time in my life, I need a headband, so much for my hundred-and-fifty-dollar haircut.* She enjoyed the briny, somewhat fishy scent as she watched the wind ruffling the seagrass, loving how carefree and lost in the moment she felt.

She jumped when a deep, resonant voice spoke up behind her.

"Nothing else on earth like it, is there? Low tide and its wonders." Seth, wearing beach pants rolled up displaying corded legs and bare feet, carried off the sexy seaman look to distraction. He picked up a sea-worn rock and skipped it over the water, which looked to be returning sandy patch by sandy patch to blanket the exposed seabed once more. "It's my favorite time of day."

He stood so close that Sloane could feel his breath softly teasing her ear. It made her break out in goosebumps. *What the hell is wrong with me?*

Sloane raised a hand to her heart. "You startled me! Just lost ten years of my life."

Seth gave a soft smile, his voice hushed, reverent, low.

Appreciative. "Sorry. I didn't mean to."

Sloane saw Joel, Janie, and Whaley excitedly splashing through the deepening water and relaxed a tad. Joel was fine. Safe. Janie seemed to be keeping a big sisterly eye on him despite the fact they were the same height. The girl impressed Sloane as being a wise old soul kind of child, and she wondered how one so young could give off such a vibe.

Sloane turned back to Seth and chuckled. "No problem. I feel like a kid." She gestured to everything around her—the beach, the sea, the birds. "This is another kind of paradise."

"Is there another kind?"

"Well, yes. There's the tropics. Tropical beaches are spectacular. Their lazy rolling waves offering tranquility and promise are exceptional." She gave a small laugh. Embarrassed. "Listen to me wax on."

A glint appeared in Seth's gaze. "Sounds poetic but tame."

She rounded on him. *Is he laughing at me? Making fun of my feelings?* "The Pacific can also be pounding. Hurtling itself fiercely against the cliffs and rocky coasts."

He looked skeptical. "The Atlantic is pretty spectacular, you know."

"Prove it."

"All right. I will."

Sloane scoffed. "I dunno. The curling waves drifting onto golden sands with palm trees swaying in the trade winds is pretty hard to beat."

"I betcha I can prove the Atlantic beats the Pacific."

She lifted a brow. "Pray tell how. From what I see, Cape Cod Bay is pretty lame . . . oops, I meant tame."

He cocked an eye at her. "Say what? Tame? Wait until you see more than the Bay. Are you sure you're up for the mighty Atlantic?"

"You know it. Bring it."

"Okay. Here's the deal. Be ready early tomorrow morning,

first light—"

She broke in. "First light? In the fog? Huh? Who are you, Captain Neptune of Davy Jones' locker?"

"I see whatcha did there. Clever. Ha, ha. I'm your pilot. I promised Joel I'd take him flying. I don't break my word. How 'bout we hit the skies, and I'll show you what trumps wussy tame tranquility."

"You're on." Sloane stomped away.

Seth had her there since he was the pilot taking them up. She grabbed Joel by the arm and attempted to brush the sand off. The task was hopeless. The grit clung to his skin, and his clothes were a mess.

Seth laughed. "Follow me. Outdoor showers this way." He bent from the waist like a figure from Louis the Fifteenth's court and waved them onward.

She could hardly turn on her heel and flounce away. The heavy sand didn't permit flouncing.

Joel used the shower. Whaley happily bounded inside, soaking his shaggy coat. He shook himself and ended up getting everybody wet—again. An apt ending for their first day on Cape Cod.

CHAPTER TEN: TOMORROW, TOMOR-ROW

Sloane needed no alarm clock, she always woke early, and this was no exception. This morning, she felt excited, bright-eyed, and bushy-tailed while applying sunscreen to her makeup routine. She paused, baffled when she smelled the delicious aroma of coffee. She hadn't made any yet. Then there was a knock at the door.

"Yoo-hoo. Coffee's ready, are you?" Seth stood behind her screen door, holding two huge cups of steaming brew. "Open up. This java won't wait. I brewed it myself." His chest puffed out like a rooster. A small paper bag dangled from his wrist like a bracelet.

Janie raced inside, calling for Joel. "You up yet? Are you a sleepyhead?" A pillow hit her, proving Joel was awake. Their screams probably woke the dead.

"Shhh, you'll wake the whole compound. Here, let me take that." She took a cup and slid the bag off his arm, sniffing. "Do I smell cinnamon?"

"Yuppa. Warm cinnamon buns fresh from the oven. Grab one. There's enough for all of us."

Janie and Joel ate theirs at the small maple table while Seth and Sloane went outside to watch the sea as they savored the yeasty concoction.

After emitting a satisfied hum, she said, "This is really good."

"Which. Bun or brew?"

69

"Both." She wiped her mouth.

His finger went to the side of her mouth, wiping a bit of frosting from the corner she must have missed. His touch burned through her, and she jerked away, swiping a napkin over the spot he cleaned to erase the feeling. As if a mere napkin could remove the fire from her skin, sizzling through her veins. She flushed and felt awkward. *I'm acting like a teenager, not an experienced woman.* She moved to the picnic table and took a huge bite to distract him and herself from her show of nerves. *It's rude to talk with a mouthful.*

Seth threw her a look that she couldn't read, but fortunately, he said nothing.

Talk about a minor miracle.

Seth helped her clean up, and she reminded the kids to use the bathroom before they left for the outing. Janie was chattering away, and Joel just smiled and nodded a lot. They decided to take Seth's minivan, which was parked near the office. Janie led the way.

Seth pressed the key fob, and the doors unlocked. The kids bounded in, and Sloane sat in the passenger seat and buckled up. She was relieved to see both children were in booster seats. They must keep an extra around for Janie's friends. *I'll have to get another for Joel's friends.* It had been too long since Joel had a playdate, so they hadn't needed a second seat.

After a short ride, they were at the Provincetown Municipal Airport. The tiny airstrip with a single hanger and small terminal reminded Sloane of her first flying lessons in Ann Arbor . . . with Seth. The winds were strong when they exited the car. Seth led them to a four-seater with *Wing It* scrawled across its wings in a red cursive font.

As a pilot herself, Sloane automatically began a walka-round, appreciating the fine form and feel of the craft. She wasn't surprised by her reflexive and strong reaction to the plane, she loved flying. Being on the apron once again and seeing the weather vane indicate the direction of the wind brought back memories — good ones.

"You remembered." Seth's quiet voice snapped her back to the present.

"I had a good teacher, and I know my stuff. An experienced pilot told me that once upon a time."

He laughed. "Did he now?"

"What makes you think the pilot was male?"

He paused, then nodded. "Touché. Anyone I know?"

"I doubt it."

Seth undid the tie-downs, and they completed the preflight requirements together. They entered the cockpit, and Sloane got the excited children into their seats. Then she automatically started going through the motions and glancing at the paperwork.

Seth cleared his throat. "I'm piloting."

She gave a nervous laugh. "Of course. Old habits . . ."

Seth winked. "I'm glad to see you haven't forgotten the rules." He began to taxi to the runway.

Sloane still found herself impressed with his precise skills and deft maneuvers. "No tower? That makes it tricky."

"No tower. The winds are the bigger challenges I find." He slanted a look at her. "Next to you and getting you to follow protocol."

As they began to climb, she blurted, "I follow protocol. You know I do."

The plane soared, and she soon saw the Atlantic beneath them. She felt the headwinds and watched as Seth centered the yoke, leveling their flight path.

Seth chuckled. "Settle yer feathers, Sloane. I'm yanking your chain."

"Why on earth would you do that?"

He winked. "Cuz I can."

Sloane glowered at his intriguing profile. His features were strong and even, and she still liked what she saw, if not what

71

she heard. *Did he have that cleft in his chin before, or am I just noticing that now?*

Seth glanced at her once the climb was over and the plane was straight and level. "What? You're so easy to rile. And it's fun to see you fuss and fume."

Sloane drew in a breath, then huffed. "I'm glad you find me amusing."

"I find you delightful." He pointed. "Look starboard, two o'clock."

She did just in time to see a whale breach.

In a rush, Sloane shouted, "Kids, see there? Whale!"

Joel's eyes rounded. "There she blows."

Janie bellowed. "Yeehaw!"

"Never gets old," Seth said. "We'll make a date to whale watch. It's one thing to see them from the air, another from the sea."

A joyful ruckus broke out from the cheap seats. "Can we? When?"

Sloane jumped in her seat. *Date? He said date. He probably didn't mean a* date *date. Did he? No. I'm being silly. He's talking whale watching with the kids. That's not a date.* "You're on! That was unbelievable. I've never seen anything like that. And the Atlantic *is* spectacular."

"You ain't seen nuthin' yet, kid." Then he banked to the right. "Hang on to your hat, but first, you need to know the basic—"

"I think by now you know I've mastered"—Sloane paused, winking—"the basics."

He chuckled and shook his head. "The basic geographical layout of Cape Cod. You'll see that the landmass forms a raised, some say flexed, right arm, spanning from the mainland east to the Atlantic Ocean. Within the curve of the landmass is Cape Cod Bay. The roads we're flying over are the main arteries. There are just a few—Six, Six-A, Twenty-eight, and my personal fav, Shore Road. Now, look. Along the

Atlantic-facing shoreline is the Cape Cod National Seashore. It stretches forty miles from the tip of the elbow near Chatham north to P-Town. It encompasses forty-three-thousand-six-hundred-some acres and includes excellent beaches, some bike trails, and several historical spots. It is part of the Massachusetts Coastal Pine Barrens ecoregion, which includes Nantucket and Martha's Vineyard. We have President John F. Kennedy to thank for establishing national status back in nineteen-sixty-one."

As they flew on, Sloane was indeed impressed by the sand dunes, marshlands, shorelines, and cliffs spreading below, making her itch to get down there to experience it all on foot. She could see the forested areas interspersed with ponds, seagrasses, beach plum blooms, and beach roses.

Sloane's hand stole over her heart, enchanted. "Ohhh, my God, it's breathtaking."

"This is just from the air, a bird's eye view. Wait till you see it up close and personal."

Sloane oohed and aahed, overwhelmed by the beauty of the land, sea, and sky. The cerulean blue of the ocean was utterly magnificent and appeared calm. She could only imagine its moods but intended to become well acquainted with them all. *This is so much more than I dreamed it'd be. I don't know what I expected to find, but this is something else.*

Seth turned the plane and headed north. A few minutes later, he pointed. "There's MacMillan Wharf. I'm gonna fly over the Wing It kiosk. Hello, P-town, here we are."

Sloane drew in a breath. "Incredible. To think we were right there yesterday! Amazing. To see this from the air is awesome."

"To your right, that tall stone structure is the Pilgrim Monument and the building with the clock tower is the Town Hall. You gotta see those on foot, too."

"Looks like there's a lot to see and do here. Was that a lighthouse we just passed?"

"Yes. Race Point Lighthouse. This is just the tip of the iceberg. We have a thriving art world, an active theater, nightlife, hiking, biking, swimming, and plenty of towns and history to see. Just you wait. The world at your fingertips."

She laughed. "I could spend a lifetime here. Now I see why Whitt wanted me to come."

He grew serious. "I know you need to talk to me about what brought you here."

Sloane swallowed.

Seth glanced at her and obviously saw she was struggling. "But not right now."

Sloane jumped in. "No. Later. This isn't the time or place." *Why was Whitt so insistent that I contact Joe? Surely not just for sightseeing.*

She didn't have time to think about what she should say because Seth was preparing for landing. As he made the approach, she noticed the sleepy little airport was a bit more active than earlier. When everyone disembarked, Sloane helped Seth complete the post-flight walkaround and tie-down process.

"We'll talk another time," Seth agreed.

From the air, Sloan had noticed the low tide draining the shoreline, temporarily marooning skiffs and other small craft moored along the beaches. As they drove back to the Inn, the kids clamored to get home faster so they could hunt for exposed treasure.

"I bet we could find pieces of eight if we look really hard," Janie announced, "We can hunt forever. The sea is way far out there. Whaley will love it."

Seth's expression didn't mirror Janie's enthusiasm. "I think he'll be happy just to see you're home. I'm sure he isn't up for another bath."

Janie giggled and poked Joel's shoulder. "You shoulda seen Whaley getting a hose bath. He tries to catch the water spray like a Frisbee. Then when he can't, he jumps up in the air—snapping his jaws like this." She used her arms to form a crocodile bite. "But he catches nuthin'."

Joel's eyes sparkled and grew rounder with each word.

"It was so funny when he got Uncle Joe all wet."

Joel appeared curious but didn't speak. A question lingered in his expression, yet unspoken.

Janie continued. "Whaley shook his whole body like he was doing the *Hokey Pokey*."

Seth—aka Uncle Joe—rolled his eyes. "Yeah. I got a full-on doggy shower I didn't need."

It took mere minutes to get to the Inn parking lot. The kids exploded out of the SUV like bullets from an AK14.

Janie issued a challenge. "Race you to low tide, Joel."

Both children made a beeline for the seashore as she and Seth walked the sidewalk toward their respective cottages, nodding hellos and greetings as they passed other guest residents.

A middle-aged man dressed in cutoffs and a fisherman's hat slapped him on the back. "Hey Joe, great to see ya."

Two women in yoga gear stretched and sang, "Jooospeh."

He gave them a namaste gesture and a smile.

It appeared Seth, aka Joe, was a popular guy. He explained that most guests stayed from Saturday to Saturday, quickly forming a community. Seth responded with quips and jokes, knowing just about everyone by name. "We watch families grow up and return with their children. Then they come back with their babies. It's really cool. Maybe you will, too."

"Who knows? I certainly don't. All I know is I am on my own now and will do my best for Joel. I'm not looking for pity or help or a handout. I will do what I must to survive and get my son raised happily. I'm not looking for miracles."

"If you don't look for them, you could miss them, ya know?"

"What I know is this. Somehow, some way, I'll get the job

ahead of me done. Don't know how or where I'll land."

"How about a happily ever after."

"Oh puh-leeze. No, thank you. I don't need—much less want—a man."

"So, you into women?"

"I don't need another *person* complicating my life. Don't need anyone full or part-time unless it's a miracle worker. Otherwise, no need . . . for anything. Not to fight my battles, not to provide for me, not to mess with my life. I'm fine as I am."

"You're young. What about having two-point-five kids and that other stuff? The mutt, the picket fence?"

"I have plenty of fences, don't need another mouth to feed. Not looking for love. It is not on my to-do list. Been there, done that. Look where that got me. Too complicated. Not interested."

"Companionship? Someone to share things with?"

Sloane quirked a brow. "Sounds like you're talking about a hound again."

Seth merely chuckled, gave her a wave, and took off toward his cabin.

As she continued down the walkway, it was clear folks around here enjoyed letting their hair down. They seemed happy and friendly, and like her, outside enjoying the warm summer breezes as much as possible. Some families were staking their canopy roofs to provide shade over their picnic tables and lounge chairs. Others started firing up their charcoal barbeque grills or were still spending the remaining daylight hours beneath their lollipop-colored umbrellas dotting the beach.

She spotted Janie and Joel walking on the boardwalk leading down to the beachfront. Janie held a pail and shovel, and Joel had the pickle jar she'd found for what he called his *sandsakes*. Sloane had grinned when Joel came up with his own version of *keepsakes*. She loved how her son made new words for old, tired concepts. While some schoolchildren were instructed to use the term *guest teacher* for substitute teachers, Joel didn't follow that convention. He called them *absititutes* — a combination of *absent*, a word heard each day during attendance counts, and *substitutes*. In the winter, he would say he had to be careful not to get *ice bites* instead of frostbite.

Once back at her cottage, she quickly slipped on a pair of flip-flops and began making her way to the shoreline. Walking on the lawn, sidewalk, and boardwalk was easy, but then she remembered how hard it would be to navigate the expanse of dry sand ahead of her. After stopping to tap the sand free from her footwear several times, she decided to carry hers by their straps. Happy that she had thought to grab her visor, she conducted her own treasure hunt lifting a pretty shell here and a glittering pebble there. She kept her movements slow and casual, a literal beach stroll. As she neared the exposed sea bottom, she dropped her shoes to walk barefoot, enjoying the feeling of the wet sand oozing between her toes.

As Sloane strolled along, she found Joel's discarded sneakers and left them to retrieve on her way back. It was obvious his Crocs didn't cut the sand either. She looked at other people's footwear and discovered the secret to their sand walks — slip-on mesh shoes. She made a mental note to buy some as soon as she could. Just a shake of the foot made the sand slip out of their sand shoes. They didn't seem to struggle to walk through the sand like she did.

The sun was nearing the horizon but had yet to color the skies. Sloane briefly closed her eyes, absorbing the briny air with the cries of happy children and feeding gulls mingling with the gentle sound of lapping waves.

Ahead of her a bit, Joel started jumping up and down, yelling. *My boy is yelling!* Beside him, Janie was dancing with excitement and pointing. Sloane noticed Seth approaching the kids from another direction and witnessed him bending down to examine what they had found.

He stood and yelled, "Dinner!" as he held up a huge, obviously recently stranded, fish. It wriggled in his grasp but was clearly not going anywhere.

Sloane caught up with the group. "What? Really? Dinner?"

"Yep, and you're invited. Striped sea bass straight from the sea. Doesn't come any fresher than this. What a catch. Come on, kids, time to scale and gut this baby."

Both kids hurried to help. Her child was apparently going to clean a fish for the first time. Come to think of it, Sloane had never done that either. She considered herself a *city girl*, not a fishwife, but she tagged along. She helped Seth spread newspaper — conveniently folded, recently delivered near his door — over the picnic table.

Seth held the fish using the gills to show Joel how to scale the bass. Sloane didn't much care for the messy process, getting hit in the eye here and there by a wayward scale, but she backed off a bit once the fish head was removed and the real cleaning began.

"Take this trowel, Joel, and dig a hole in the seagrass over there to bury the guts," Seth instructed. "Janie, you bury the head in our garden."

Janie grumbled. "Why can't Joel do it? He's the rookie."

He cocked an eye at her. "Seriously? Company, remember? You know the drill. Give back to Mother Nature. Do your bit. On your way, please check the coals on the grill. Let me know if they're white or not." Then he glanced at her. "I started the coals for dinner before joining you on the beach. Was going to fix burgers, but this is too good to resist. Hope you like fish."

Sloane grinned. "Grilled fresh striped sea bass? What's not to like?"

The sun streaked the sky with gold and red as their savory supper was grilled over smoking coals. Sloane added sweet corn and foil-wrapped potatoes to complete their dinner.

Seth plated the fish, bowing as he handed her one. "At your service, madame. Bon appétit."

"Chef's special?"

"Oui."

Sloane took a bite. Smiled and said, "This is. The. Best. Fish. Ever." She licked her fingers. After they were full and satisfied, she rounded up the kids. "K-P duty, kidlets. Take these plates inside and prepare to wipe dishes."

Joel groaned.

Janie looked up. "What's K-P?"

"Kitchen patrol. You can be my S-A-D."

Janie gave her the stink eye. "Is that a fancy word for chores, cuz it sounds a lot like work."

Sloane raised a brow. "What? Sergeant at Dishtowel? A very serious job."

Seth chuckled. "Is that a thing?"

She poked him back. "Shh. It is now."

As they worked, she heard a commotion outside. The sun had long set, so what was the deal? Curious, she peered through the window and saw a stream of folks heading beachward.

"Where is everyone going? Sunset's over."

Seth carried a bottle of wine and two glasses. He smiled and gestured to the screen door. "Step outside with me."

Sloane did and immediately understood the draw. The Milky Way spilled across the sky in a spectacular display she knew she would never forget. Light pollution blocked the starlight at home, but there was not enough light nearby to dilute this splendor, the wonder of the starry sky.

Joel came up next to her and gasped. "What's that?"

Seth's voice boomed through the quiet. "That's the Milky Way, son."

"I'm not your son! I don't have a dad anymore." Joel raced

away down the beach.

Sloane was too shocked to move.

Seth spread his hands out—still clutching the wine and glasses—a look of confusion on his face. "What'd I say?"

Janie spoke up. "I got this, Uncle Joe." She whistled. "Whaley fetch. Get Joel." She turned to Sloane and winked. "He'll be fine."

Whaley followed Joel at a run, and Janie chased after him, calling over her shoulder, "Don't worry, Miss Sloane, Joel won't get very far. Whaley will kiss him to death."

Dog and boy tussled, rolling on the grass.

Janie grinned. "See what I mean? Told ya."

By the time Sloane and Seth caught up, Joel was clearly over his fit. Whaley had him giggling as he said, "Get off me, Godzilla dog. Off."

The kids from the other cottages called Janie to join them. She gestured for Joel to *come on*, and the two ran off.

Sloane opened her mouth to speak when Seth said, "Not to worry. Each night all the kids roam the compound playing. The older ones watch the younger ones."

Her skepticism must have shown because Seth went on. "Besides, the sprinklers come on at ten, and all the kids automatically return to their cottages."

Sloane huffed a small laugh. "Like the streetlights coming on when we were kids?"

Seth smiled. "Yeah. Like that." He handed the wineglass to Sloane and pointed to the bonfire pit.

The pit was circled with weathered benches and down a ways from the row of cottages. Far enough for privacy and fire prevention yet close enough to keep an eye on things.

Seth selected a bench away from the others. He leaned close as they sat and whispered, "You can let out that breath you're holding."

"What?"

"Relax. Everything's all right. Joel's fine." He removed the cork from the wine bottle. "Try this."

Sloane shivered despite the hoodie she had thrown on and held out her glass. "I don't know if I'll ever relax again. I haven't had a moment to chill since Whitt died."

Concern crossed Seth's features, but warmth shone in his gaze. "This would be a good time to talk about that."

She nodded. "Yes, it would, but I don't even know where to start." The firelight provided a perfect setting to let the sea and sky take over.

Seth winked. "I find starting at the beginning helps."

Sloane gave a small laugh and nodded. "After I left Ann Arbor—"

"We don't have to go that far back. Sloane, I know we parted under . . . Well, you don't have to go there."

Sloane sighed. "It's time, Seth. I up and left with no explanation."

"Only if you say so. As far as I'm concerned, the past is the past. It can stay there."

She laughed again. "Oh yeah? The past is never done with us, though, is it?"

Sloane began again. "When I left Ann Arbor, I had to go home to take care of my mother, who had a massive stroke causing a car accident. I didn't know whether she'd make it through. Her care consumed me. I couldn't think of anything but her and her care. In the process, I met Whitt at WSU. At first, he was just a distraction, but he hooked me up with his father's firm to handle Mom's finances. I didn't know anything about Roth IRAs, annuities, stocks, and mutual funds. I don't know much more now. Whitt took care of all that when we married."

"That explains your recent problems."

"Yes. In short, he handled the money."

"You did have your hands *full*, ya know."

Her voice wobbled. "Be that as it may, Whitt was charming, steady, calm . . . It wasn't a surprise that I began to rely on him. He was older, ahead of me in school, working on his MBA. We ran into each other — literally — at the student union building. I plowed into him crying, and the rest is history. I was barely twenty-one . . . didn't know much."

"Not to mention he was a stud." His remarks broke the building tension.

She giggled. "He was."

"Fundamentally, my buddy Wittman was a good guy." Seth winked. There was a gleam in his eyes. "He had good taste. He married you. He always did step up to the plate."

Sloane smiled softly. "He did. Formidable in business and so confident, but he struck out big time, I'd say. I didn't know then that he . . . He was . . . slippery, hard to pin down. He'd blow me off when I wanted to discuss things."

"Oh, yeah, he knew his shit, but that's part of the issue, isn't it? He knew his stuff but got caught up in it, too."

"Something like that, yes. To make a long story short, it was more than enough that he died, but he took my son, my job, and my dreams with him."

Seth looked her in the eyes. "Only if you let him."

She bristled. "Easy for you to say. You're not the one with the selectively mute son.

"No, but I am the one left with a broken-hearted *tween* and a rollickingly shaggy dog, so I have an idea of life's curveballs. By the way, Joel talks. I've overheard conversations—"

"What?"

"Between him and Whaley."

Sloane couldn't stop the frustration and sadness that colored her words. "My point exactly. Occasionally, he'll talk. When he wants to. He's been mostly silent or screaming up a storm." Her hands twisted in her lap. "For the longest time, Joel wouldn't talk to me, his teachers, or even his therapist.

82

We couldn't get a word out of him."

"Hmm, he's talking plenty now, though."

She nodded. "Since this trip."

"Looks like you've given him something to talk about. You can get all of it back, ya know."

Sloane stared at him as if he were nuts. "Oh, can you raise the dead now? I'm not sure I want Whitt back. I'm pretty pissed off with him. He left us in a lurch."

Seth grimaced and muttered. "How did he die?"

"Coronavirus."

"Good Grief! At his age?"

Sloane nodded. "Underlying conditions, which he ignored. He worked straight through the COVID shutdowns and took chances. Didn't listen. Didn't get vaccinated. Whatever they said to do, well, he didn't. Said old people got it, and it was just the flu. Said he was young, fit, and healthy. But it got him, and he left me holding the bag. When he died, I lost everything." She paused, her throat clogged with a storm of emotions. "You have your job. I don't. Many of my clients came through Whitt's connections, and they got bilked. They bailed on me after his debacle."

"How bad off did he leave you?"

"Bad enough that I'm here looking for Joe Blow."

He chuckled. "You got the *B* right. Bradford, not Blow."

"You know what I mean."

"I do, and that's the trouble."

She looked at him. "Why did he send me to you? What can you do?"

Seth turned deadly serious. "Help out. Rescue you. Give you a way through or a way out."

"That'll be the day! No one rescues me," she snapped.

Seth tilted his head. "But I do, though, don't I? I came to your rescue at that Party of the Century, didn't I?"

Sloane felt her temperature rising, and with the heat of a

nuclear bomb, she said, "I don't need to be rescued, and if I do, I'll rescue myself. I've put on my big girl panties and can deal. Thank you very much—for nothing. I don't know what Whitt was thinking. I don't see how you could possibly help. You were too late before, and you're too late now." She downed the rest of her wine and left him sitting by the fire, mouth gaping and looking as stupid as she hoped he felt.

CHAPTER ELEVEN: MORNING HAS SPOKEN

Sloane made coffee and took the thick crockery cup outside along with her sketch pad, wanting to capture the beauty and peace of the morning. The light was what she mentally called sea light. The rising sun colored the water with the early morning striated clouds collecting the pinks, lavenders, and peaches. The effect was very different from Michigan's often pearly pewter or lead-gray skies at best.

Here on Cape Cod, Sloane could use pastels, making quick swoops to catch the bands of hues. She was utterly captivated by the contrasting sand and sea grasses and loved how the light lit the beach roses. Noticing Whaley and Janie scouring the beach off in the distance, she sketched them as part of the composition. She drew Janie's ponytail trailing behind her like a kite in the sea breeze, and her hot pink outfit added more color to the sketch and mirrored those of the sky.

Sloane looked up from her work when Joel stirred and brought his cereal outside. "Be careful. Don't slop on my sketch."

Joel made a growly sound and moved further down the table.

She set her work aside and ruffled his hair. "Are you Mr. Grumpypants this fine morning? Did you forget that we're going to Race Point to see what we shall see?"

He pushed her hand away but said nothing.

Sloane bit her tongue, deciding enough was said.

85

Hopefully, the wind would blow his cares away like it did for her. They got ready for the day, and she continued sketching while Joel made tunnels and canals in the sand.

Whaley bounded over as if heaven-sent and woofed. The dog circled them, barking. Sloane got the idea that he wanted them to follow. Hoping she was right, she gestured to Joel, and they followed. Whaley led them to the Bradford cottage.

"Good Boy, Whaley. Good fetch." Seth ruffled the dog's fur, then turned to her. "Ready to settle things?" His tone held a bit of challenge.

Whaley woofed and took off.

Sloane matched his tone. "I may be — it depends. Settle my future? What's to settle?"

"The Battle of the Century."

"Oh that? You mean the Battle of the Sexes. That's over. Done. Fini."

Seth spoke as he loaded the minivan. "Oh? How so? Who won?"

"I'm surprised you haven't figured it out by now."

"Enlighten me, m'lady. Pray tell."

She cleared her throat. "It's algebraic. Simple math . . . and hormones."

"If you say so, but you haven't explained how." He grinned.

Sloane used her most succinct tone. "Women have two X chromosomes."

"So, I've heard."

"Men have only one. Plus, they have a Y. And . . . that's *why* they lost. *Two* Xs beats *one*."

He raised his baseball hat and scratched his head. "The Battle of the Oceans is easier to win. You ready?"

"Bring it."

"Think we should bring the ragamuffins?"

Whaley barked again. They took that as a *yes* and piled Joel and Janie into the minivan. Whaley tried to hop in, too, but his huge brown puppy dog eyes didn't cut it this time.

Seth drove straight down Shore Road and turned onto Route 6, which was as close to an expressway as the Outer Cape got. A short trek by car led them through pine-dotted dunes. The scrub forest roadway was a gateway to the sea. Two thin white cirrus clouds crisscrossed, forming an X in the sky.

Janie spotted them. "Look, there's a ginormous cross in the sky."

Joel squinted. "Looks like a big X to me."

Sloane chuckled with a wide grin. "X marks the spot. Proof that women rule." She pointed to the clouds. "God just gave us a sign."

"But," Seth said, "I predict the Atlantic will win *our* contest."

"We shall see."

They walked down a sand dune path leading to Race Point Beach. Sloane stopped in her tracks. Never had she seen anything like this. The roiling sea crashed into the shore in a pounding rush of deep colors. Greens in the waves met whites. Black waves joined blue. The wind captured the sea and crashed into shore as if it was angry. Huge ocean swells hit the shore only to recede and race in again from seemingly different directions—all at once. Its energy sizzled through her being. She was hooked.

The Atlantic held her in its thrall, greeting her like a puppy dog. The sound and fury, the foam and spray, fit her like her own skin. She prayed she could paint what she felt and saw. *Does it make Seth feel this way?*

Her fears fell from her psyche as if they had never consumed her. The ocean rocked her world like no man ever had.

Sloane took one look at the surge of water and felt its energy. Its might. She felt joy. *Joy? Definitely. It makes me want to scream and shout.* So, she threw her head back, tilted her face to the sun, and twirled.

In the background, she saw the kids joining her and Seth clapping and smiling. But they were not her focus. *Being.* Just *being* was the thing. *Being joyous* in this sea space. Happy in her head space for a change.

Sloane inhaled deeply. She didn't dare exhale lest she lose any part of the sea's power. She couldn't speak. The Atlantic overwhelmed her. Her fingers itched to capture it in every media at her disposal—oil, charcoal, pastel, and watercolor.

The sea was alive. Alive like she was. The wind caressed her face when it blew her hood back. She stood there like a figurehead mermaid, making no effort to put it back in place. There was nothing tame about this. Shakespeare's words— *Faulkner perhaps?*—ran through her mind. Sounds of sound and fury but signifying everything in her version.

CHAPTER TWELVE: I SAW HER FACE

Seth knew he'd won the stupid bet. But in that moment, he knew something much more was happening within Sloane. He saw it in her face. Something in Sloane had settled.

Sloane looked beautiful standing there. The sea breeze blew back her platinum blonde hair, revealing a face that was laughing, crying, and probably praying from what he knew of her. Her expression paid homage to the pure unadulterated energy that made the roaring Atlantic, the Atlantic.

She didn't seem to notice when he walked to her side. When he slipped his hand in hers, she didn't pull away. Then he shared what she must be feeling as it surged through him, too. Something magnificent and magical filled him with happiness and awareness, and he—in ways he could never articulate—saw the ocean anew through her eyes. She appeared more regal than he remembered, more graceful than he thought a woman of her stature could be.

Seth didn't feel a need to goad her into a response. Didn't need to tease her. Didn't need to provoke her. What she gave him in that revealing moment was a glimpse into what made Sloane who she was and who she was becoming.

He saw the girl he remembered with new eyes. Before him stood a woman. *Was she this fierce back then? Yeah, she was fearless. A force to be reckoned with.* A product of the nature that forged her. She was no victim. No wonder she snapped at him when he was stupid enough to suggest a rescue attempt.

Sloane was right. She did not need to be rescued. Her whole being shouted that to anyone with eyes and ears. Her

89

regal stance told without words that she was ready and willing to take on the world. So, what does she want? He wasn't sure, but he wanted to be the man who delivered it.

Janie ran up to them with Joel in her wake. "Joel's hungry. Can we take him to Sunday School? Puh-leeze."

A confused look crossed Joel's face. "It's Friday."

"Every day is Sunday around here." Janie sang. "You'll see."

"You like Sunday School?" Joel's incredulous expression indicated his doubt of Janie's sanity.

Janie nodded with vigor. "I adore Sundae School. You will too."

"I don't think so. I hate Sunday School. Boring. Mom, do I hafta go?"

Sloane tore her attention from the sea and looked at her son. "Uh, yes, don't be a party pooper. Seth's the driver, he calls the shots."

"Good call, Miss Sloane." Janie practically bounced in place.

Seth chuckled. "Joel's hungry? We can't have that. To Sundae School, then." He winked. "Hope it's still open."

Joel grumbled. "I hope it's not."

As much as Seth wanted to stay in that moment at Race Point, the day had gotten away from them, and the drive to obtain food would take a while, so still holding Sloane's hand, he led them back to the parking lot.

Joel and Janie raced past them, climbing the dune instead of the proper pathway. They made it to the top before he and Sloane, but not without effort. Climbing a sand dune wasn't easy and was against the rules and regs. Seth winced as Joel pulled himself up using handfuls of seagrass—also against the regulations. Luckily the beach police weren't nearby because there were fines for going off the path. At the top, both children collapsed dramatically, laughing. He resisted the teachable ecology moment. What's done is done. He knew he could work the lesson in sooner or later.

Seth cupped his hands and yelled, "Last one to the car is a rotten egg."

The kids shot back to the car like bullets.

The drive through Cape Cod National Shoreline reminded Seth they were in an expansive national park. Many stretches offered forests, scrub pines, sand dunes, bike trails, hiking paths, and museums.

Sloane said, "I'd like to come back and paint this. And Race Point Beach, for sure." She grabbed her phone and took picture after picture.

Seth enjoyed seeing her so relaxed and at ease. As they traveled on Route 6, Seth pointed out the way to various beaches giving bits of fun facts and directions should Sloane decide to venture out. "Cape Cod has all you need. All but skyscrapers and city smog. We do get traffic congestion and must stay alert for the darn bikes on the road. Those and narrow roads create traffic issues." He pointed to the many people on bikes on both sides of the road. "It's high season, so we get more traffic jams but look at the scenery. There are marshes, kettle ponds—"

Sloane frowned. "Kettle ponds?"

Seth responded, using his travel guide voice. "Yup. That's what they're called. As the scribes say, *They were originally formed by melting blocks of ice that left depressions in the landscape that eventually filled up with fresh water.* There are about a thousand kettle ponds throughout Cape Cod. So, the ponds are isolated bodies of water like bowls of soup sitting in the landscape. We have cranberry bogs, beaches, and historic buildings. Like I said before, Cape Cod has it all."

About forty minutes later, they reached Main Street in East Harwich, where a charming shop stood with a sign reading *Sundae School Ice Cream.* As he parked in front of the shop, he noticed Sloane checking out the enlarged newspaper clippings posted on the bay window. One claimed *Best Ice Cream Shop in the United States* by *Food and Wine Magazine*, and another by *USA Today*, stating *Rated 5th in the Country*.

Janie started jumping in her seat, squealing. "See why I love it?"

Joel pumped an arm. "Yes."

Seth explained, "Sundae School was started in nineteen-seventy-six by a schoolteacher and his wife, who needed a way to afford to spend their summers here. So, they opened the ice cream parlor, serving up homemade ice cream — made to order in small batches. Exciting flavors. And it's delicious."

The kids clapped and squealed.

Seth glanced at Sloane. "You up for sharing a Super Sundae?"

"You know it."

"Since you're a first-timer, you get to choose the flavors . . ."

Sloane smiled. "How nice."

" . . . as long as they are Amaretto, Bass River Mud, and Buttercrunch." He grinned as they walked into the shop.

"Hmm. I see." Sloane laughed. "Can I get a cherry and nuts and whipped cream?"

"You can have a nice big Bing cherry on top with a side of bananas. Want crushed walnuts or almonds?"

"Yes." She smiled.

Janie nudged Joel and pointed at the menu board. "Try the Shark Tooth. It's wicked."

Joel looked at the picture Janie pointed to and gaped. "Look, Mom, there's white chocolate triangle *teeth* in it. But don't worry, this ice cream isn't real blood. It's raspberry, I think."

Janie giggled. "It's blackberry blood. Eeww."

Seth ordered for everyone, and Sloane grabbed napkins.

They took their orders outside, walking behind the shop to the tucked-in patio with picnic tables and umbrellas. It was the perfect place to enjoy their ice cream. Small trees, flowering bushes, and a bubbling birdbath fountain added a hominess to the place.

Seth teased back and forth with Sloane, arguing over who got to eat which flavor. The kids giggled at them while they enjoyed their own confection.

"You sure fooled us. Right, Joel?" Sloane chuckled. "Imagine having a sundae in Sunday School. Quite clever."

"Now that you've finished your sundae, you can call yourself a graduate," Seth added, "of Sundae School."

Sloane sang sardonically. "Pretty clever. Yuck, yuck, and all that." She turned to Joel to clean off his face and hands, then offered Janie hand sanitizer before they got back in the car.

Seth grinned as he drove them in an easy silence if she discounted Janie's steady stream of commentary. It seemed Janie was as talkative as Joel was quiet.

Her mouth turned down a bit, and she sighed, knowing under normal circumstances, Joel would have chattered away as well. Then she reminded herself that Seth had made a good point. Cape Cod certainly had enough new and exciting things to do and much to talk about. She settled back and enjoyed the view out her window.

The peace and quiet were interrupted by Joel's cry. "Fire. Giant floaties. On the roof! Can we stop, Mr. Joe?"

Seth threw her a look that said, *make way for super-sized floaties.* He smiled, stopping the minivan, getting out, and eyeing the top of his vehicle.

Sloane groaned, knowing sooner rather than later, she'd have a huge inflatable on her hands. She looked out at the variety of humongous hot pink flamingos, aqua mermaids, green dragons, and what-have-you anchored on the roof of *Seabury Souvenir Shack.*

The kids bolted out of the car, and Sloane followed at a slower rate. It took only seconds for Joel to lug an inflated alligator to the register.

She laughed. "There are no gators here or flamingos, for that matter. Are you sure you don't want a shark?"

In response, Joel shook his head. She sighed, which turned into a laugh as Janie chose a Unicorn, and Seth lugged a huge banana sundae floaty big enough for two to the check-out counter.

The clerk handed her a ball of twine so they could bind the trio to the minivan. Her body brushed against Seth more than once as they struggled to tie down the floaties. Seth's solid warmth hit her like a woman waking from a case of amnesia in Antarctica. A longing she hadn't felt in years swamped her. Desire swept through her like wildfire. She nearly felt bereft when they succeeded with the tie-down and no longer touched. She ached to jump his bones.

She shook her head. She wasn't used to thinking like that, and it scared her. Love was not on her to-do list, and sex shouldn't be either. She wasn't a horny teenager, for heaven's sake, and had way too many problems without dealing with the complications of sex. However, her self-chastisement didn't slow down the desire zinging through her body in the least.

Seth looked thoughtful, then drawled, "I know the perfect place to try these out."

Sloane's "huh?" was drowned out by the yays and yeses of the excited kids in the back seat. She held her breath, worried about safety, sharks, and the wild ocean. Visions of Race Point's crazy seas were fresh in her mind.

Janie took a guess. "Herring Cove Beach, Uncle Joe?"

"Something better."

After a few moments, Seth turned into the Bradford Sail

Inn and parked. Sloane slumped in her seat with relief. *The pool.*

Seth smiled. "I promise I will keep the kids—and us—shark and riptide free. Janie isn't sea safe yet either."

She smiled. "Sea safe is a thing?"

"It oughta be."

Joel and Janie jumped out and headed for the cottages. Whaley greeted them with his usual enthusiasm and sloppy kisses. The kids—on a mission to use their new floaties—ignored Whaley and hurried to change into their swimsuits, leaving her and Seth to wrestle with the inflatables. Seth carried the sundae-for-two while Sloane tackled the others. Once they wedged the inflatables between lawn chairs, they went to change as well.

Sloane wore her teal tank suit and threw on a cover-up. She hurried back to the pool to keep an eye on the kids.

Seth walked out wearing a nice pair of board shorts that displayed his solid, perfectly muscled abs and legs. The waist sat low on his hips, drawing her eyes down to the dark hairs leading to the slight bulge. It increased in size when she took off her cover-up. *I think I got a rise out of him.*

Getting wet was one thing—the pool was not heated—but it was another to try and climb onto their floaties. Joel's laughter was loud and joyous. When he and Janie tried and failed too many times to count, he was exuberantly beside himself.

Sloane had no better luck. The vinyl squeaked, protesting her repeated attempts to get inside the culprit. Each try chaffed not only her skin but also her ego.

Seth's grin spoke volumes, but he reached out. "Here, grab my hand. I'll help you."

Laughing at herself as much as anyone, she grabbed his hand and hopped to assist but landed in a very unladylike position, flat on top of him. She quickly moved over, toppling them. Whipping her dripping hair off her face, she helped right the craft, but the rubber groaned, and her fingers slipped when she tried to hold on. When she got her laughter under control, Seth somehow managed to get inside and reached out to her. She ignored Seth's extended hand, grabbed hold of the floaty, and tried again—and failed . . . again. *If Seth can manage to smugly perch inside the stupid piece of shit, I can do it, too.*

Sloane grabbed the edges of the inflatable contraption, only to upend the whole thing, dumping her and Seth. This time though, they ended up entangled in a hot full-on body press, driving her senses insane with desire.

After they got the thing upright again, Whaley chose to join the fray and leapt inside, flipping the whole thing and sliding into the water. Meantime, the floaty escaped to the opposite end of the pool.

Sloane was thankful Seth had thought of the pool instead of the beach. Even the gentle Cape Cod Bay would have proved hazardous with all the slip-sliding failures they experienced.

In desperation, Seth grabbed her ass and thrust her over the edge into the center of the sundae. She scooted over as the children shoved Seth inside, which landed him on top of her. His hands wandered, groping for purchase, sweeping across her breasts and privates. Her girlie parts sizzled when he settled with his package pressed against her. The floaty rocked, and they tried to stabilize it when the kids torpedoed it across the water, which caused the stupid thing to flip, tossing them into the drink again. She came up sputtering and laughing so hard she could hardly breathe. *I haven't had this much fun in a long time.*

Seth smiled. "Looks like someone needs rescue breathing. Good thing I am a certified lifeguard."

The sundae ship was on its side, blocking them from prying eyes. Seth's lips found hers with a quick, devastating kiss that left her gasping.

He looked at her. And winked. "What?"

She blushed. *I don't want the kiss to end.*

Chapter Thirteen: Every Now and Then I Fall Apart

Sloane shoved the silly floaty away, and Janie and Joel commandeered it, with about as much success getting inside as the adults. Seth dragged Whaley out of the pool and sent him on his way. Whaley promptly shook himself, rolled on the beach grass, then lay down for an afternoon nap. Sloane retreated to a lounge chair, put her feet up, shut her eyes, savoring the afternoon sun on her skin, and slipped into a light doze as she listened to the kids play. They were fine.

"Marco." Joel's voice sang in the breeze.

"Polo," Janie answered.

"Marco."

"Polo."

The back-and-forth chant would normally drive her nuts, but she was too happy that Joel was acting like a typical kid, not the traumatized child of recent days. She was caught by surprise with the sudden urgent, irritated tone of Janie's voice.

"No fair hiding under the floaties, Janie called out. "Come out, come out wherever you are. Marco. Marco? Marco! Answer me."

Sloane jolted upright, screaming, "Joel, stop playing around. Answer me, young man." She couldn't see him. Not anywhere, but then she noticed the sundae floaty overturned.

Seth must have seen something because he suddenly dove into the pool and surfaced a few moments later, lifting Joel to the side of the pool.

Joel looked pale and limp.

"Joel! Baby!" Her heart was pounding in her chest. "Oh, God. God."

Seth checked Joel's pulse, then rolled him onto his side. Joel started to cough, and Sloane started to cry. Joel coughed up water and gasped until he was breathing easily again. He was alive.

"He's okay, Sloane," Seth said. "He's breathing. It's okay."

Sloane marched to her son's side and looked at Seth, who looked rather pale himself. "Nothing's okay, Seth. He could have died—"

Seth quickly grabbed her shoulders and barked, "He didn't. Stop that kind of talk." He slanted a glance at Joel. "You're okay, aren't you, son?"

Sloane felt her body slump. Seth was right. Joel was alive but shaken. She placed a towel around Joel's shoulders.

Joel began to shake as he glared at Seth. "I told you. You're not my dad."

Seth got down to Joel's eye level. "No, I'm not. I wish I was so your pain could go away. No one can ever take your dad's place. I can't, that's for sure, but what I can do is show you the things he liked to do when he was your age. That might help some."

Whaley bounded toward Joel as he walked away. In seconds, the big goofy dog tackled him and gave him drooly kisses.

Janie watched the drama unfold around her with eyes rounded with shock, surprise, and concern. "Miss Sloane, let Whaley take care of Joel. He knows what to do. Plus, Whaley's a very good listener."

Sloane nodded and took her at her word. "Thank you, Janie, Seth. We've had enough fun for the day."

On legs that felt as feeble as cooked noodles, Sloane made

her way back to her cottage. Joel was wrestling with the big shaggy angel, Whaley, and seemed no worse for the wear. *That dog is heaven-sent.*

She and Joel walked to the food truck. Joel ordered a cup of clam chowder, but her stomach was too upset to try to eat. They went back to their cottage and sat at the picnic table. She wasn't up for the low tide homage, nor was Joel.

Later, when Janie and the other kids began their nightly romps, Sloane was happy to see Joel join in.

As the sun stained the sky in glorious reds, she sat in the Adirondack chair, appreciating the view and filled with gratitude. *So glad I came here. Whitt was right. There's magic here. I feel it all around me.*

Seth joined her, carrying a bottle of wine in a lighthouse-shaped bottle. "I find when things are heavy, you should drink twice as heavily."

She chuckled. "Not sure that's the answer, but who am I to argue?"

He poured her a glass.

She sipped it. "This is good."

He nodded. "It's locally produced at the Truro Vineyards."

She looked at her wine. "This has an interesting taste. I don't recognize it."

"It's cranberry. The vineyard has a tour. It's up the road. You passed it on the way here."

She shrugged. "Must have missed it. I think you're pulling my leg again, buddy."

He grinned. "Big wine barrel in the sky marks the place."

He chuckled when she looked at him blankly and said, "No? Don't recall that?"

She grinned and threw her hands up. "Hey, Joel and I managed to lose Niagara Falls, so I'm not surprised we missed a little old wine barrel."

He threw his head back and laughed. "I bet there's a story

there. I can't get you to the falls, but how about we find that honkin' wine barrel?"

"Now?"

He smiled. "It's closed for the day. So, no, not now. How about tomorrow?"

She clicked her glass to his and made a toast. "Here's to the Vineyard. Yo, Truro, we're coming."

Sloane surprised herself and relaxed. She had yet to fully emerge from the onslaught of emotions brought on by Joel's close encounter with the pool. Her hand shook slightly as she raised the wineglass to her lips again and again.

Seth teased. "You're about to drain Cape Cod Bay if you keep that pace up much longer,"

She raised a brow. "Fetch another bottle, if you please."

To say she was giddy was like saying the ocean was deep. She was weak with relief. Truth be told, she was more than slightly buzzed. The tension of the preceding year with Whitt's death, the reporters, the public scandal, the loss of her job, shame, the sleepless nights, and the worry over her future was enough. Joel's selective mutism was a whole 'nother kettle of fish, but the kicker had been Joel's near drowning. She took a deep breath as she envisioned Seth lifting Joel from the pool, looking so little, pale, and wan. If she didn't watch it, she'd dissolve into a puddle. She glanced at Seth. *Make those two puddles.* One of tears and another of molten hot want and needy desire.

The winds were chilly, and she drew closer to Seth's warmth. The next thing she knew, her lips were on his, and her hot pool of raw need overflowed. Her tongue explored Seth's lips, flicked over his teeth, and played with his hot wet mouth. His response kicked hers into overdrive.

Seth moved away, and Sloane shivered.

She looked up at him. "Whas happenin'? Where you goin'?"

He pulled her gently to her feet. She swayed into his body, and his arms supported her as they made their way toward the cottage door.

"Woman, what is it with you? Why do drugs — in this case, cranberry wine — bring out the wild woman in you?"

She stopped and drew him back to her. "Huh?"

He chuckled. "Come on, sugar. It's been a long day. The sprinklers are on, and the kids are comin' home to roost. Let's get you back."

"Baby, don't go . . ." His face swam in her vision.

He whispered in her ear, "Tomorrow's another day."

Joel reached them, took a quick look, and said, "Last one in bed is a . . ." And he went off like a shot in the dark.

Seth slipped Sloane's water shoes off, making her wobble and start to topple. He scooped her into his arms.

"Déjà vu," she slurred.

He carried her over the threshold like he had in the past.

She giggled. "I do, again."

Seth agreed and tucked her into bed, covering her with a sheet. "Shh," he said, warning Joel to be quiet when he noticed Joel staring with big, wide eyes.

Sloane heard their soft voices through her wine haze.

"Your mom won. She beat you to bed." Seth dropped a kiss on her head.

Joel plopped onto his bed.

Seth tucked him in and turned out the light.

Joel squeaked, "No dark."

Seth left the kitchen light on.

Joel quieted and settled down.

CHAPTER FOURTEEN: I NEED YOUR LOVE

The caw of the seagulls sounded like sirens. Sloane awoke and started to rise. The room tilted, and she sank back into bed with a groan. Joel's footsteps sounded like a basketball thrown against the wall. Her stomach protested, and she felt like hell. She shoved herself to her feet once more and staggered to the bathroom, where she hurled the contents of the hellfire wine from a lighthouse-shaped bottle in several heaving bursts. She leaned against the putrid porcelain and felt like dying for the second time in her life. *How humiliating.*

Joel must have heard her and came rushing to her side. "Mom, you're throwing up blood! You need help."

Before she could speak, he took off at a run. *Great. Just great. He's calling out the cavalry. And that means Seth.*

Joel knew he needed help. He ran to Janie's cottage to get Mr. Joe. Whaley barked like crazy, scratching at their door.

Janie opened it. "What's wrong, Joel? You look like a ghost."

"Mom's puking blood. Where's Mr. Joe? I need him."

"You and me both." Janie sighed and held up a lighthouse-shaped wine bottle. "What do you think Uncle Joe's doing?"

Joel heard Mr. Joe somewhere upstairs, hurling like his mom did.

Janie winced. "This calls for Aunt Monalisa. She has some

secret sauce."

"Huh?"

"It's something that stops people from . . ." She opened her mouth, stuck her finger in, and made a gagging sound.

"Ohhh. I get it."

An irritated voice accompanied the footsteps pounding down the stairs. "What in tarnation is all the ruckus about?"

Aunt Monalisa shuffled into the kitchen. "Joel? What are you doing here?" Her gaze fell on the empty wine bottle, and she turned to Janie and nodded. "I see." She used the blender to mix some ingredients—Gatorade, something that looked like more wine, tomato juice, and a packet of powder. She jerked her head to the bathroom and said, "When your hungover uncle emerges from the throne room, make him drink this." She pointed to the concoction. "If he doesn't, give him this." She poured some wine into a juice glass.

Joel scrunched his face. "Eww. What is it? Looks like wine."

"Also known as the *Hair of the Dog.*"

"Isn't that what made him sick in the first place?"

She winked. "Sometimes what hurts ya cures ya. The trick is the amount you drink in the first place. Take it easy. Drink not so much, and viola, you're cured."

Joel's gaze went instantly to Whaley's fur. Whaley woofed, and Joel shook his head. He reached out to take the glass.

Aunt Monalisa frowned and held the glass back. "Hmm, I better take this to your mom. You kids stay here and keep an eye on Uncle Joe's recovery, hear? Be sure he drinks that."

Sloane heard the screen door slam and covered her ears. Why was everything so damn loud? She dared to open one eye to see if it was her worst nightmare come true—Seth. *Please, God, don't let it be Seth. Anyone but Seth.* She sighed when Monalisa

Bradford stepped into the bathroom.

Monalisa turned on the shower, helped her to stand, and whisked off her sleep dress, then shoved her under the spray.

Sloane winced and yelped. The ice-cold water made her skin goosebump. She hung her head and tried to steady herself but couldn't stand it for long. She emerged grateful for the robe and the drink Monalisa handed her.

"Tsk, tsk. Look at you. Two peas in a pod. The pair of you. Sicker than a dog who ate a beached whale left in the sun for a week. Think you'd know better by now, but apparently not. From the tales Mallory told . . . history's repeating itself, no?"

Sloane adopted a rueful tone. "Better it's *you* mopping me up this time rather than Seth."

"Oh, he's no saint, for sure, and if it makes you feel any better, he's in the same mess. Seems like he's led you into it— again."

"Not his fault. Either time. I'm a big girl. And I was then, too." Sloane shocked herself by admitting she no longer held Seth responsible. Or accountable. For either time. *Son of a gun.*

Monalisa chuckled. "No doubt about it, you'll both be nursing that hangover all day. I'm taking the kids down to low tide, and I'll feed them too while you and Seth get your act together."

Sloane mumbled her thanks as she led the way to the kitchen.

Monalisa moved toward the table when Sloane's open sketchbook caught her eye. "This is good. You draw these?" She rifled through the pages that featured Cape Cod Bay, outlining streamers of clouds, sea birds, and beach.

Sloane's cheeks heated. "Yes, I dabble a bit." She'd spent a long time pouring over sketches of sand, water, and sea froth.

"These should be done in oil."

Sloane nodded. "That's my next step. I'm surprised you see it that way, too. Why is that?"

Monalisa laughed. "There's a huge thriving art colony here, and I'm part of it. *Mona Lisa Bradford Incorporated* at your service."

Sloane gaped in shock. "*Thee* Mona Lisa Bradford?"

A twinkle lit Monalisa's eyes, and with a sweep and graceful bow, she said, "In the flesh. Or I should say, in my pajamas."

Monalisa headed for the front door, seeming to sway just a tad, but Sloane wasn't sure if she wasn't the wobbly one.

As Monalisa opened the door, she threw a comment over her shoulder, "Thank you for not laughing at my moniker."

"You're welcome, but why would I laugh at your name?"

Monalisa turned to face her. "My parents were artists. They had a sense of humor, so they saddled me with Mona Lisa. I combined it into one word, but I capitalize on it with my public persona, as you'll notice when you see my signage."

Sloane was beside herself. Even in her present hungover state, she perked up. "The Mona Lisa Bradford Gallery? In P-town?"

Monalisa nodded. "Oh, there's another one in Wellfleet near Uncle Tim's Bridge. A smaller one. White weathered wood, black shuttered cottage. Used to belong to some old sea captain. You need to check it out while you're here. That one is known as *Ole Paint Gallery.*"

Sloane laughed. "Seems you have a sense of humor, too."

"Wait and see. There's more, but I won't spoil it by telling you now." Monalisa snapped her fingers. "I got it. I'll meet you there. And before you protest too much, I'll pack up the kids and a picnic lunch."

Sloane's arm crossed her belly, and her hand stole across her mouth. At the mere mention of food, her stomach churned.

Monalisa continued. "The kids will enjoy exploring Duck Creek and the marsh. I'll tell Seth to get on the stick and take you, so you can see the gallery."

Sloane's face heated again. "I have a car."

"Parking is at a premium. Seth has a parking permit. You wanna carry all that stuff? The easel, the canvas, the paints? Plus, stopping to pay the fee and get a permit? Why?"

"Huh?"

"Get your act together, kiddo. You'll need your *art* supplies so you can translate your sketches to canvas, capisce?" Monalisa cocked a brow. "Come on now. I've got eyes. That's a lot to lug and tug when there's a hunka burning man who can do the grunt work. You'd pass up the opportunity to have some help? Really?" Her look was piercing, and a shrewd expression crossed her face. "Methinks you and Joe have some unfinished business to conduct. Gotta do it somewhere, why not there? Shed some daylight on your history, dust off the past, face the future. Without the wine this time. Your load hasn't been easy. I saw the newspapers. I hear Whitt sent you here to talk to Joe. So, get on with it."

Sloane gaped, too stunned to do more than nod. She grabbed her phone to pull up her artwork. "Damn. No signal."

Monalisa raised a shaking hand to her head. "No matter. If they're anything near as good as these, send for them pronto. That is if you want to sell them." Monalisa peered over her half glasses. "In my gallery."

She couldn't keep her incredulity from her voice. "Do I! That's a yes."

Suddenly, she felt better, even though the drink in her hand tasted tart, tangy, and not so good. She took a deep breath and blurted, "I'm scared."

Monalisa nodded. "Of course you are. Facing the past and charting the future would frighten the best of us."

Sloane shook her head. "That too, but it's more than that. I can paint Michigan lakes and catch the magic, but what if I can't reproduce this?" She spread her hands to indicate the area outside. "The essence of the sea. The color. The light. The energy. The excitement."

Monalisa raised a single finger. There was a slight shake in it. "Only one way to find out. Paint. Just paint. Channel what you just told me. Paint *that*. Tell me what supplies you need."

To Sloane's horror, she could feel hot blood throbbing in her veins. *Holy shit. She sees right through me.* "Thank you. I don't mean to impose . . ."

Monalisa huffed, then stated in a firm tone, "As a woman, I see it as a duty, a sacred obligation to support and assist other women in any way they need for them to succeed."

Sloane stared into Monalisa's eyes and saw that she truly meant what she said. "Wow. Just wow. But you're sure this isn't an *I feel sorry for the poor widow with a child* thingy?"

Monalisa straightened. She filled her lungs and then released her words. "That's as close to an insult as I have ever had, my dear. I don't put just anything in my gallery unless it's worthy. My offer isn't a handout or even a hand-up. It's simply good business."

As Monalisa was leaving, she looked back over her shoulder, "Oh, and I'll be happy to share what I know about capturing the sea but let's see whatcha got first. You may not need my input."

Sloane drained the glass. "Thanks for this, too. What's it called?"

Monalisa laughed, nodding her head. "Your *Seth* calls it Monalisa's Special Sauce. I call it *Hair of the Dog Plus*." She paused and threw in for good measure. "I hope you and Seth wake up and smell the coffee. Stop pussyfooting around and foolin' with fire. There're several things ya do with fire. Douse it, fuel it, or bank it. I suggest you do us all a favor and fan it into flames. Take care of business." She fanned her face. "The radiant heat is burning the rest of us. Take him to bed. Make a damn move."

Sloane's cheeks felt like they were on fire, well, that and her girlie parts. "Uh, I think I already did. Last night."

"Do tell. I want deets." Monalisa chuckled.

Sloane waved her hands to discharge her nervous energy. "He might as well have said no."

"Did he say no?"

"He said tomorrow's another day." She giggled.

Monalisa shook her finger at Sloane. "Today *is* tomorrow. Take your shot. Everybody can see he's stuck on you."

Sloane's mouth opened in a huge circle.

Monalisa winked. "Shut yer mouth, sweetie. Sugar catches flies, doncha know. My work here is done. Buck up, buttercup." She waved and headed down the walkway.

Sloane flipped through her sketches of low tide, the detritus of the sea, the clouds and drift line, where the seaweed dried after the tide deposited it. She tried to picture the colors she'd use.

She knew she'd labor over creating just the right colors. The pewters of the sea in the evening, the indigos of the approaching night sky reflecting purple then black as night spilled across the water. The browns of the seaweed, whites of the shells, and the blacks of the sea birds. She planned to paint the speckled, black-bellied plovers. Or were they killdeer? Or sandpiper? *Hmm.*

She remembered they passed *A Bird Watchers General Store* on Route 6 in Orleans. She noticed it on the way home the other day. Birds intrigued her. *Bet I can get a field guide there. It will make my color choices accurate. A variety of seabirds on the beach with driftwood would make a vibrant seascape, providing I get the colors right.*

Sloane donned her visor and bathing suit, then covered herself with a large sleeveless *Save the Whales* t-shirt. She tied a windbreaker around her waist and grabbed her sketch pad and tote bag on her way out. She plopped into a lawn chair

109

waiting for her on the patio.

"Whatcha got there, Picasso?" Seth wore a baseball cap and aviator sunglasses. He groaned and slumped into the lawn chair next to her, glancing at her sketch pad.

She grinned. "Actually, I'm more of a charcoal Wentworth wannabe."

Seth peered at the page. "Where'd ya find that huge hermit crab shell? I didn't notice that."

"I found it in my mind's eye. Sometimes you have to coax the brain and exercise the imagination so it matches the picture I see in my head."

He scratched his chin. "It'd be pretty interesting getting into your head."

Sloane slanted a look at him. "Hmm. I'm surprised. Not what I expected to hear."

"Huh? Why? What did you think I'd say?"

She lifted a brow and took a breath. "Most men would say something about getting into my bed or pants."

Seth winked. "Not this one." He paused, and his forehead creased. "Not that those aren't good ideas. Just because I didn't say those words doesn't mean I didn't think them." He leaned forward in his chair and brushed a light kiss on her lips. "Days a-wastin', and we have a date."

She leaned back and looked at him. "We do? What date?"

Seth shook his head and threw his hands out in mock exasperation. "Last night, before we got under the influence, we made a date to go to Truro Vineyard's Wine Tasting. You ready?"

Sloane gulped and felt the color leave her face. "I think not. Not a good idea. More wine? Uh-uh." She slumped into the chair, suddenly feeling her head and belly swim.

Something he must have felt, too, because he suddenly pitched forward in his seat and lowered his head between his knees.

Hope he doesn't hurl. If he does, I'll join him.

110

He straightened. "Yeah. That sounds about right. Another time then?"

Nodding in agreement, she asked, "How is it that I only get high or drunk when you're around?"

"I must be a bad influence on you somehow or other. Hmm."

"If it quacks like a duck, walks like a duck, and flies like a duck . . . it's a duck. You are a big, bad influence on me, sir."

He shrugged. "Tell me you're not hung over?"

She grinned. "Well . . ."

Then he stopped and held a hand to his forehead. "Wait a minute. Did you make a pass at me? Last night? And I blew it?"

Sloane grinned. "Maybe. But I think not. It probably was a wine hallucination, or maybe the *pass* of which you speak was merely in your dreams."

"I insist on a do-over."

She laughed. "Some other time." *We've come full circle. What's good for the goose is good for the gander.*

Seth paused, looking around them. Sloane followed his gaze and noticed some guests were up and about. The others milled around setting up sunroofs, tents, and bright, colorful umbrellas, yelling hellos and greetings their way.

Seth tilted his head, then snapped his fingers. "I got it. Change of venue is what we need. A day on the beach, a cat nap . . ."

Sloane sat up. "I dunno. Monalisa suggested we check out her gallery near Uncle Tom's Boardwalk."

He grinned. "Bridge. Uncle Tim's Bridge."

"Whatever." Sloane stood, shifting from foot to foot. "She said she'd meet us there with the kids and a picnic. We, uh, I could see the gallery and then check out the area, maybe paint some. Make the day special or at least better than we feel."

"You lookin' special, not so green as you were earlier."

"Seriously? That's the best you got?"

111

He threw his hands out. "I got more than that. I have an easel, pallet, enough paint to sink the *Whydah* – "

"Whatsa a whyda?"

"The *Whydah*, my dear girl, is a pirate ship that sunk in this neck of the woods, uh, sea about three hundred years ago."

"You're pulling my leg."

Seth held a leg out. "My pegleg?"

"Very funny."

"It's true. There's a museum and everything on MacMillan Wharf. We can take the kids some time." He slapped his forehead. "My brain is under strain. I can't keep it straight. Let's see. We get over this hangover. Go to the gallery. Meet the kids at Uncle Tim's Bridge. Paint. Picnic. Right?"

"Yes, but first we need coffee, lotsa coffee." Sloane went inside and returned shortly with two steaming mugs.

Seth took the brew. "Monalisa said we can use her Paint by Number – "

Sloane's mouth hung open. "Excuse me? What?"

"She calls her van *Paint by Number*. It's a converted airstream for artists. It's a mobile art studio specially modified to go over sand, hill, and dale. It has everything you'll need. You know what I mean?"

She laughed. "This I gotta see.

"And so you shall after we get you ready for the day."

Sloane looked herself over. "I am ready. As ready as I'll ever be."

"I beg to differ." He reached into his cargo shorts, pulled out sunscreen, and began applying it to her arms and exposed shoulders in long, hot strokes.

His touch ignited her blood in the process. Sloane drew in a quick breath, knowing she would win a bet that her eyes were bright as a flame in the night, reflecting her heat. It looked like he just might kiss her. She hoped he would. Then his finger – moist with sunscreen – traced the rim of her ear.

112

First one. Then the other. His touch melted her.

He dabbed some sunscreen on the tip of her nose. "There. Missed a spot."

He totally broke the mood.

She shrugged, a tad irritated with herself and him for not acting on the vibe and stealing a kiss. She stomped off — not masking her irritation — toward the parking lot, leaving him in her wake.

"Wait up. What'd I do?"

"Nuthin'. That's what you did. Not. A. Thing."

"What did I miss?"

Sloane turned to him so fast he crashed into her smashing her breasts into his chest. "This." She kissed him hard. "And this." She kissed him again.

He leaned into her and murmured, "But I didn't miss this." And then he took over and really kissed her.

The kiss was everything and more. Hot and wet. Hard but soft. Fast but not. Long but too short. Then Whaley careened around the cottage and crashed into them, breaking them apart.

Janie, fast on Whaley's heels, started singsong, "Uncle Joe and Miss Sloane sitting in a tree. k-i-s-s-i-n-g."

Monalisa, trailing Janie, asked, "What's all this racket about? Down Whaley. Sit." She was dressed for the day, wearing water shoes, beach wear, and a well-used candy-pink sunhat complete with a mesh neck flap designed to prevent sunburn.

With the sun as hot as it was, Sloane forgave Seth for ending their prior exchange with his silly action because he may have prevented a nasty burn to her — it turned out — extremely sensitive ears. *Did I always have such responsive ears?* She couldn't remember what Whitt did or didn't do to them. He certainly never did *that.*

Monalisa and the children took off in Seth's van. Sloane

followed Seth into the most remarkable vehicle she'd ever seen. An old-fashioned aluminum recreational trailer on monster truck wheels that had the words *Paint by Number* written across both side panels. Numbers in every size, color, and shape decorated the rest of it. She hoped it had a fold-out awning and something like a portable dance floor, too. If it did, her easel wouldn't dip.

CHAPTER FIFTEEN: IF A PICTURE PAINTS A THOUSAND WORDS

Tension slipped from Sloane's shoulders as she sat in the passenger seat of the huge vehicle. The folks nearby pointed and joked as Seth pulled Paint by Number out of the lot onto Shore Road, heading to Route 6 toward Wellfleet. He slipped a David Gates CD into the player as they drove. She inhaled the scent of the salty breeze through the open windows, drank in the sight of pitch pines lining the sides of the road, and soaked in the scenery all around.

The roadside beach shacks they passed sold souvenirs, jelly, beachwear, and Lord only knew what else. Sloane observed the weathered gray shingles of the beachfront cottages, the aqua-green sheen of the ocean, and the red and white buoys hung out with tan nets to dry. Her inner artist took notes, paying close attention to the many hues so she could reproduce them on canvas.

The sea breeze contained more than salt. It held a wisp of magic—a flash of something she could not name but felt like the positive vibes of promise and possibility. Whatever it was, she welcomed it and intended to seize its essence and include it in her paintings.

Sloane watched the quaint cottages flash by. They made a pretty picture, but each stood for more than their looks. They were a testimony that though things changed, and raw nature assailed them with rain, wind, and fierce storms, they still stood strong and tough. She saw them as a metaphor. If they

115

could withstand the raw elements of nature, she could too. Mistakes and missteps could be repaired, sins forgiven. The island stood the test of time, and deep within, she knew she just might, too. Her duty was to protect Joel, and by God, she would. *It's okay to be a teensy-weensy bit scared of the task, though, right?*

In her mind's eye, she pictured herself at Race Point facing the mighty ocean, the wind blowing through her hair, throwing caution to the wayside, standing her ground, hurling her worries into the pitching waves. She smiled. *That's some self-portrait, all right.*

Seth broke the silence. "You're quiet. Still hung over?"

"Kinda, but I'm a bit better since I drank the *Kool-Aid*."

"*Kool-Aid*?"

Sloane winked, then chuckled. "Monalisa's secret sauce." She grinned as she gazed out the window. "This place does sumthin' to ya, doesn't it? Hooks ya like flying does, wouldn't you say?"

Seth cast a glance at her. "I suppose so. Never saw it quite that way before, but yeah, the sea does have its own *tug*."

She coughed, her hand covering her mouth to stifle a laugh. "Ahem, before you ask, yes, I *caught* what you did there, you clever captain. Maybe you missed your calling and should *pilot* a fishing boat."

He puffed out his chest, looking pleased with himself. He paused a bit, then said, "The sea does hold the same rush. Both bring the same kind of peace, but flying fits me like a condom."

Sloane burst out laughing. "Not the comparison I was expecting."

Seth winked. "That's the point, isn't it?"

"Huh?"

"Rubbers cover everything, so you won't be *expecting* anything."

She swatted at him. "You ruined my poetry with your

116

imagery."

"I didn't know you wrote poetry."

"I don't. I paint it." Then she switched gears and adopted a deliberate dreamy tone. "The sea brings two things into play. Energy and excitement. And yet it somehow remains peaceful. It's a sense of timelessness with forever soaring vibes." She grumbled and shook her head. "I can't define it. Can't get the words to match the feeling." Her fingers flexed, itching to hold a brush.

"Then paint it."

"How do you paint magic?"

"I don't know, but if anyone can, it's you."

Sloane smiled. "That's the plan."

Seth pulled in and parked behind a two-story former sea captain's house, identified by the distinctive gold and black schooner plaque. It had apparently been repurposed somewhere along the line.

Seth helped her out of the paint mobile and led her around to the front steps. A sign planted in the sparse grass read *Ole Paint Gallery, Mona Lisa Bradford Proprietress.*

"Prepare to be dazzled." Seth winked as he opened the door.

The beautiful display of artwork inside the period piece home transformed it into a true art gallery. Sloane ran her hand over the heavily carved furniture—most likely brought home from the sea captain's voyages around the world—that gave a nod to the age of the home.

She noted the furniture stood perfectly spaced among the oil seascapes. Juxtaposed with those were various abstract artworks with colors of the sea. These vied with still-life compositions. Vivid emerald greens played with streams of amethyst, sapphire, and aquamarine. She loved using those colors in her own work.

Watercolors stood sentry, flanking the archways between

rooms. Porcelains and china figurines on pedestals and tabletops stood next to embossed leather trunks. Jade carvings were strewn throughout the house. Sloane glanced at everything with an artist's critical eye, feasting on the ambiance around her.

She yearned to live among this treasure trove. How fun to collect them. Display them. Place them. To *have* them, even if only for temporary ownership. To be able to provide them for others to enjoy. *Looks like a perfect job to me.*

Each room contained uniquely exquisite art perfectly arranged for the best showing. *I must have died and gone to artist heaven.* Sloane knew everything was available for purchase, which only increased her regard for Monalisa Bradford and the care she took to pull everything together so other people could wrap themselves in this beauty.

A small parlor with walls painted in sea blue awaited a new exhibit. The sign on a small easel near the entrance read *Coming Soon. Guest Artist.* She wondered whose work it would feature—*mine maybe? I can see my acrylics on these stands. The tree collection would work here, too. My Lake Michigan canvases would pop next to them. I've got to get Addie to include my Lighthouse Collection. A girl can dream, right? Monalisa wasn't joking. She told me to get my work here.* Sloane whipped out her cell and texted Addie.

Send my paintings and Lighthouse series to Bradford Sail Inn. ASAP. Thnx.

She included a heart emoji for good measure.

Sloane could spend a month or a lifetime perusing this house and its treasures. She had never seen a gallery like this one. Addie's gallery was nice but much more formal. Ole Paint Gallery offered hominess and comfort.

While she wandered from piece to piece, Monalisa came inside. She clutched at the wall, steadying herself. Seth conferred with his aunt for a bit. Monalisa nodded, wagged her fingers, and made her getaway. Sloane could hear Whaley barking outside, and judging by the cries of the kids, she figured they were playing fetch. The hubbub faded. No doubt Monalisa had corralled Joel and Janie to take them to the bridge.

CHAPTER SIXTEEN: STILL STANDING

Seth saw the range of emotions playing across Sloane's face as she wandered around the gallery. It reminded him of when he took her to Race Point. He wished he'd taken a picture of her looking at that sea to show her what he saw while watching her—a tall, strong, courageous woman taking on the world. During their time together, he suspected she had no clue that she was as mighty as the waves pounding the shore and not fragile by any means. It seemed so wrong for that feisty, fearless, spunky pilot he'd known in the past to lose her bearing, not by her own actions but because of the outrageous actions of Whitt and his many mistakes.

It was clear to Seth that the close call Joel had experienced in the pool made another huge assault on her psyche. He saw it in how her face had paled, her trembling hands, and her demeanor. *Hell, her pain hurts me.* But he also saw her fight back and stand tall. *I'd like to know where I stand with her.*

Whenever Seth witnessed Sloane's tenderness with his independent niece, it got to him. When Janie needed Sloane's attention to fix her hair, adjust a strap, or tie a bow, Sloane complied with gentleness and affection. Likewise, Seth noted her exhilaration when Joel spoke or acted like a typical young boy. *So much to like about that woman.* Her response to beauty was a turn-on, too. He kept discovering new depths in her that he had not witnessed when he flew with her in the past. He was also amazed to uncover new dimensions in *himself* just by being around her.

From Sloane's expression, traces of the spunk he remembered existed. But that was tempered and refined now, banked like a bonfire waiting to ignite. *Passion. That's what I'm seeing. A passionate woman. Definitely not simply the gal I knew. This is Sloane version two-point-O.* His man parts perked up just watching her wandering through the gallery. And he felt something else equally strong too. Desire. Want. Need. Lust. Tenderness. All of that roiled inside his boxer briefs. *Down boy.*

Once he got his rod under control, he asked, "You about ready to head out, Sloane?"

She drew herself up. "I guess so. Ready, Freddy. Let's go."

Seth held the door for her and happily followed the sway of her hips as she walked by. After talking to his aunt, he took her suggestion and headed to Race Point.

Monalisa and the kids were going to Uncle Tim's Bridge to explore Hamblen Island and Duck Creek. He prayed Sloane would forgive him for his change of plans. He started the engine and set off.

He reached High Head and made the turn onto Cape Cod National Seashore's Oversand Route. He stopped briefly to adjust the tire pressure and continued. The path wound through the sand dunes until it opened onto the beach. He had to keep an eye out for the wildlife. The nesting season was probably over, but the birds typically stuck around until September.

Sloane's raised brows and the delight in her smile when she spotted the ocean made him release the breath he didn't realize he was holding.

"Where's the bridge?"

"Change of plans. Hope you don't mind my executive decision, but Aunt Monalisa could see your fingers fidgeting in the gallery and figured you must be itching to paint. She suggested she take the kids to the bridge so you and I could come here. Do you mind?"

She looked him square in the eye. "No. But be sure to discuss any future decisions involving my kid and me. I trust

Uncle Tim's is a safe place to be and that Monalisa can handle them. Otherwise, there would have been trouble with this Mama bear."

"Trust me. They're in good hands. Uncle Tim's a lot less dangerous than Six Flags."

"There's a Six Flags around these parts?"

"In Springfield off I 90, but that's a far cry from Uncle Tim's Bridge. I'd never suggest an amusement park without you and your ability to corral those kids. Don't think I can do that by my lonesome." He parked on the back-beach—a zone so-called because it was back far enough to miss the high tide line. He had already checked the tide charts and knew they'd be okay for a while. He positioned the Paint by Number bus to protect Sloane's painting equipment from the wind while still permitting a perfect view of the beach, dunes, and the sea.

Sloane nodded. "Good. Nature works for me and trumps any amusement park, in my opinion."

Seth agreed. He loved being outside in the elements, too. To him, the sea was like a second sky. Anything sky-worthy got his approval. "I bet Six Flags would get Joel *talking*, though."

Sloane laughed. "Screaming wildly, whining, and begging doesn't count for talking."

Seth began unloading the bus. He undid the attachments from the side, then assembled the flooring and adjusted the motorized awning so the blazing hot sun wouldn't blind her.

Seth stripped down to his swim trunks and extracted the sunscreen from his cargo pocket as Sloane removed her cover-up. With his gaze locked on Sloane's curves, he spread the lotion over his chest, belly, and arms but struggled to reach his back.

Sloane approached and took the tube, squeezed a good portion of it onto her palm, and said, "Let me help with that."

He almost laughed when she stood on her toes to reach his

shoulder blades. His six-foot-five height was still a stretch for her, so he squatted to her level.

Sloane's hands spreading the warmed oil over his upper back made him tremble. Her touch raised goosebumps, and it wasn't even chilly, let alone cold. On the contrary, it felt like she was spreading molten lava . . . or at least hot honey.

Her ministrations lingered over his biceps, making him anticipate her hands on his abs . . . and lower. Shivers chased each other up and down his spine. Her fingers traced over his hip bones as she moved the waistband of his bathing suit to slather more lotion there.

Finally, he couldn't take it anymore. He bolted to his feet and grabbed the oil. "Your turn."

Seth decided to return the favor, hoping his touch provoked a similar response in her. He moved so fast that Sloane had no choice but to let him. Her skin was soft and silken. He smiled as she squirmed when he made circular motions between her shoulder blades. She gasped when he touched the strip of exposed skin between the top and the bottoms of her swimwear. He stilled his hands and looked at her over her shoulder.

She tilted her head. "What's the matter? Do you want me to burn like a red-breasted tern?"

He laughed. "No, we wouldn't want that. But a red-breasted tern? I don't think they're a thing."

Her look teased, practically offering an invitation. "Maybe not, but there are sunburns, and that I don't want." She smiled. "Bring it."

"No problem. Sounds like a plan. Just trying to be politically correct."

She looked at him with a befuddled expression, but he jumped in before she could ask. "You know, inappropriate touching."

"I'm hardly jailbait. We're consenting adults."

He chuckled. "So, we are. Good to know."

His touch lingered, becoming a caress as he took his time to apply the sunscreen. He covered every lush inch of Sloane that lay exposed, but *he* was the one burning when he finished. And not from the sun, but rather due to her, her heat, her consent, and her occasional glances that set him on fire. The noises she made sounded like a kitten's purr. He noticed her gaze fall to his crotch, which jolted in response.

She noticed and winked. "Tell me what you really think."

What he thought was he'd like to act on that consent she talked about earlier. ASAP. But he couldn't—not yet.

However, as soon as Sloane entered the paint mobile to gather her supplies from the day bed, his crotch tightened even more at the mere sight of her movements. Despite telling himself to wait, he just could not.

He followed her inside, took the canvases from her arms, and wrapped his around her. The fire between them couldn't be fought any longer. He kissed her. His hands roamed her sun-lotioned skin as he lifted her top off her sleek slender body.

He groaned when Sloane met his fire with her own. Her fingers tip-toed down his torso, untied the swim trunks, and shoved the fabric down his legs. His rod sprang up like a jack-in-a-box, and he felt himself leaking when her hands fondled him.

Seth half-carried, half-lifted her onto the daybed, and his limbs had a mind of their own as he lay beside her. Her hands explored, too, twining, joining them together, and driving him insane. He could feel her wetness against his thigh, they clearly didn't need much foreplay. With a groan, he fumbled through his shorts, looking for a condom. Sloane returned his wet, deep, open-mouth kisses, took the foil packet from his hand, tore it with her teeth, and put it on him. He was hot, willing, and more than ready. It sure looked like she was as well.

Sloane's legs wrapped around his waist, pulling him deep inside her inferno. They rocked together hard and fast, and he quickly lost all control. Her moans of pleasure rocked him to his very soul, and he roared as he came inside her hot core.

Her climax was the best sound he ever heard. No sea song could top the aria of her passion, at least for him.

Their coming together was more than a simple romp in the sack, but what it was exactly, he didn't know but welcomed it and wanted more. After a moment, their combined body heat made them pull apart, panting but satisfied.

He found a towelette on the shelf holding paint and cleaning supplies and handed it to her. "Hopefully, this will help. A shower would be preferable, undoubtedly. We can use the outdoor beach shower, but then you'd need more sunscreen."

She laughed and took the wipe. "Thanks. But we both know what that would lead to."

He grinned. "Yeah, but you love the beach, etcetera, etcetera . . ." He waggled his brows. "It'd be an ideal place to get laid."

She pulled on her bathing suit bottom. "Not now."

"So, outdoor sex isn't your thing?"

"Maybe some night it'll be the right time and place." She laughed and began putting on her swimsuit top. "The real question is, did I pick the right man?"

He winked. "Your reaction and climax suggest you did. Tell me what you really want, woman."

She giggled. "I think I just did."

He hmphed. "All you had to do was ask."

"Hmm, about that. I asked three times, maybe more."

"You were high, remember?"

She flounced away, throwing her words over her shoulder as she turned to regather the supplies. "I consented."

He threw her a serious look. "Under the influence."

Sloane shrugged. "Consent's consent."

Seth shook his head. "No, it's not. Consent isn't a contract, even when you're naked. It's a mutual thing for fully functional folks. I want *you* with all your faculties functioning." He tweaked her nose. "Then I can, at the least, blow your mind properly."

"Well, alrighty then. Perfect."

Seth helped get everything set up so she could paint. He was surprised that she seemed to be bursting with energy. He just wanted to sleep.

So, with the task completed, Seth set up a separate canopy tent and added two beach chairs beneath, then sat back to enjoy watching the sea and sun. It wasn't long before his eyes were drawn seaward. He tracked the progress of a perky plover constructing a nest in the nearby sand and beachgrass.

Nesting season was officially over, but this plover obviously got a late start. Seth would have to be careful when they left. There were penalties for disturbing the nest sites. Suddenly a 30-foot spray shooting skyward from the water caught his attention.

He quickly stood, grabbed Sloane's arm, and pointed. "Look, whale!" The beautiful animal breached, revealing its identity as a huge humpback.

She gasped and spoke with reverence. "Aww. How cool is that."

A shadow in the sea next to the whale suggested a calf.

Sloane pointed. "Oh my God, is that a baby?"

"Looks like it. Today's your lucky day."

She winked. "I'll say."

He laughed. *She's a fox.*

They watched the whale and calf breach again with mutual admiration. Seth sank back into his beach chair and relaxed to the sound of nature's heartbeat as the surf roared in and rushed out in a soothing rhythm. He cast his gaze at Sloane's silhouette. *I'd like to get her under me again and move in and out . . . slower and longer next time.* After a bit, the fresh salty air made him sleepy. He dozed.

The sound of voices roused him from a dream of Sloane's hot center. Her long legs. Her high, firm breasts. Her tight ass. The nearby chattering shattered the glorious vision with talk about the artist's work.

Seth glanced over, unsure of what to expect. But it was the portrait Sloane made, standing there so absorbed in her task, that stopped him in his tracks — had he been walking, that is.

He admired the determination Sloane displayed as she mixed hues and applied the paints in expansive brush strokes. Her concentration was phenomenal, and he was impressed with how she captured the sea with mere paint and canvas.

He fell right smack into the scene she created. Her use of color made real the slightest suggestion of a sailboat, clouds, and possible storm — a storm not truly evident. Did that reveal some inner turmoil she faced? He didn't doubt it. She had a lot to deal with. More than once, she'd stated that she had gone from a soccer mom to a single mom in a heartbeat.

Seth had a pretty good idea of what that was like when he found Janie and Whaley in his care. One day he was a single guy, the next, he was a single uncle trying to father Janie and handle a big ole overgrown puppy.

She started another painting that hinted at a whale's blow spray, and on the far side of the canvas, the essence of a fishing boat with nets outflung on either side of the vessel. Seth was amazed at how a few quick strokes of her brush conveyed so much.

A powerful picture took shape before his eyes with a few deft swipes. The result was mesmerizing. A color would lead his gaze one way, and then another shade led to still another intriguing arrangement of color and form. He got lost in the artistry for long periods as another hint of color would lead him to find something else hidden within the work. He wanted that painting for the renovations he was planning at Bradford Sail Inn.

It seemed like Sloane's hands were on autopilot. The images materialized before his eyes as if the ocean hurled itself onto the canvas. He swore he could feel the ocean foam, salty white spray, and gritty tan sand like he was part of the painted surf. He could not look away.

Apparently, Sloane was lost to the world. It didn't seem to faze or bother her that he was there. That he saw her work. That children drifted over. That their parents complimented her. That the seabirds cawed and screamed and chased each other to and fro.

Just as the tide began to go out, she stopped and sank into the beach chair after resting her brush and pallet on a tray table. She sighed, then smiled.

"Wow, lady, just wow." Seth grimaced when reality rolled in with the sun's hot rays directly overhead, bearing down on them. "Want something to drink?"

Sloane wiped a hand across her brow, leaving a slight trail of gray paint. "Not if it's hard lemonade or cider."

He chuckled. "I should have mentioned I only have water, but it's cold."

"Let me at it."

He handed her a bottle from the cooler, then used his fingers, wet from the condensation on the water bottle, to clean away the path of paint across her forehead. She jerked at his touch, which ignited something inside him worth exploring— again and again.

Sloane giggled but didn't move away. "Messy me. Artist at work. Occupational hazard." She nodded but stayed quiet as if returning slowly from far, far away. After a minute, she looked up at the sun. "Looks like we missed lunch."

Seth took that as his cue to begin rolling the awning up, capping paint tubes, and battening down the whole kit and caboodle.

Sloane moved slowly toward the paint mobile as if she was freeing herself from a trance but unsuccessfully. She took a deep breath, and her words were soft. "I need a minute." She stopped once more and turned to face the sea again. She seemed to inhale the view to store it within her.

"I can't get enough either." *Little does she know, it's her I can't get enough of.*

"Maybe we're not 'posed to. It's magnificent. Magic. Ever-changing."

He agreed. "Yup. It never fails. It hooks ya."

Her stomach growled. "I'm starved."

He grinned. "So, I hear. How about an Uncle Tim's linner."

She chuckled. "Linner?"

"A meal you have before dinner after ya missed lunch. Kinda like brunch only later in the day." He opened the passenger door, and Sloane slipped into the seat. As he got behind the steering wheel, he noticed she held her sketchpad. Although she sat still, her hands were not idle. She made quick sketches as he drove. *How many sketchpads does she go through in a week?*

Sloane did not stop drawing even when Seth stopped the paint mobile.

"Time to exit and hike it to Uncle Tim's, Sloane."

She grinned, complied, and exited but still carried her sketchpad as they crossed the street to the weathered wooden footbridge. "What a different vibe this has."

Seth enjoyed the sight as well. "This section can be a wetland when the rains fall or a meadow when the sun shines hard and hot, other times not."

Sea plants grew alongside the sign explaining the variety of wildlife they could expect once they crossed the bridge.

129

Every now and then, Sloane stopped to sketch. She pointed out how the marsh grasses grew together in bunches in natural polka dots throughout the estuary.

When Sloane stopped several yards ahead, Seth looked out at the clear view of Wellfleet Harbor, then back at her. "Are you going to paint that scene?"

"Quite possibly. Those sailboats look so peaceful and colorful, their sails billowing in the sea breeze contrasting with the sky and harbor." She looked as if she was taking a mental snapshot.

Seth imagined he'd see it in a painting or sketch sometime sooner rather than later. Her hands danced across her sketchpad. *Wouldn't mind those fingers dancing over me.*

Ahead lay the islet teaming with grasses, terns, beach, cedar pines, sea life, and sand cranes. The temperature was mild, and for that, he was grateful. "This hike is a bitch in the heat. Thank God today's weather is perfect." Nevertheless, sunburn was a distinct possibility. He made a note to reapply the sunscreen.

Once they crossed the bridge, they walked to the right along the shore. It didn't take a detective to find their group. Footprints—canine and human—in the wet hardpack sand provided clues. Whaley's barks and the children's laughter led them around the bend to spot the picnicking bunch. Seth hoped there'd be enough food left over for Sloane and him. Whaley bounded toward them, nearly knocking their feet from under them.

"Down boy." Seth bent to pick up a stick and threw it, hoping to distract the pooch so they could eat in peace. "Fetch boy."

Whaley bounded off and brought it back.

"Who's a good boy, huh?" Seth ruffled the dog's ears and saw Joel running over. "Your turn," he said, handing the stick to Joel.

Seth grinned, watching the zany mutt leap into action. "That dog has enough energy to supply Cape Cod, I swear."

Seth laughed as Sloane paid homage to the hound when he came bounding back.

Monalisa patted the blanket, inviting them to sit and eat.

Sloane finally set her sketch pad aside and accepted the plate Monalisa handed her. She took a bite. "This potato salad tastes homemade."

Monalisa smiled and nodded. "It is. Enjoy, and there's brownies for dessert. How'd you like *Ole Paint?*"

"Don't get me started . . . what's not to like?"

"You're welcome there any time. Don't make yourself a stranger."

Seth wiped his hands on a napkin. "Who are you planning on featuring this month in the parlor?"

Monalisa grinned. "Haven't decided—yet. Several new painters come to mind. Time will tell. Why don't you check on the kids? I'll take care of this stuff."

Seth's gaze followed Sloane's as she watched the children walking toward a sand bar. Each carried a plastic pail. One pail was blue, the other red. He had to admit they made a pretty picture, and Sloane's hands moved to sketch it.

Monalisa noticed and laughed. "I color-coded the pails, so there'll be no arguing later over whose is whose. Plus, it makes a nice composition, does it not?"

Sloane winked and then sashayed her way to join the kids.

Seth held back a bit. He had to get the circus in his pants under control. He made a beeline to the sea. Just in time, too, because the tide was rapidly reclaiming the seabed, and his trunks now sported a tent.

Sloane's voice rang loud and clear. "Last one there is . . ."

Had he been closer, he would have dunked her in the ocean. As it was, he immersed himself in the cool surf, hoping to tame the rising beast between his thighs.

CHAPTER SEVENTEEN: SUMMER BREEZE

Sloane wished they were alone so Seth could explore *her* the way the children were exploring the beach. As the kids wandered around, Sloane recalled the sweet sensation of Seth's hands applying sunscreen over her skin. She hoped her skin felt as good to him as his hands had when he spread the lotion over her body.

"Sick!" Joel raised something in his hands, and Janie and Whaley rushed to his side, their feet rippling the returning sea. "G'way Whaley. This isn't for dogs."

Sloane looked in Joel's small hands, where sea bits glittered. She reached for one and held it up to the light. "This one looks like it caught a slice of sunset."

Janie danced a little jig. "Wow. Sea jewels. Let me see."

Seth joined then. "Whatcha got there, buddy?"

"Sea jewels, Uncle Joe," Janie said. "Give me one, Joel. Please. Pretty please."

"Uh-uh. Finders keepers. You can see them. Later."

Sloane was thrilled to see the excitement in Joel's eyes. "What—pray tell—are sea jewels?"

"Treasure." Joel held the precious sea bits up out of Janie's reach. "Probably, ruby and sapphire. I betcha there's a shipwreck nearby."

Seth pinched a tiny piece between strong fingers and held it to the sun. "Janie calls sea glass sea jewels. This one's ruby red. It's sea glass, all right." He made a show of inspecting another fragment. "Ah yes, my guess is this one's been in the ocean for a while."

Sloane frowned. "How do you know?"

"Most likely, this is an old *Milk of Magnesia* bottle When it was glass. Today it comes in plastic. This is sapphire, an honest-to-goodness real true sea gem if I've ever seen one. Pirates can't steal these. The owner is the sea."

"What do you mean?" Sloane asked.

Once the children were out of hearing range, Seth explained. "Any piece of broken glass that makes its way into the ocean gets tossed, turned, and refined by the churning sea and sand. If the glass is in the ocean long enough, the edges are worn away and polished hence sea glass, aka Janie's sea jewels."

"Sea jewels. Love her thinking. Beats sea glass any day. "Glass," she giggled, "as crass as it sounds. They should make jewelry from them."

"They do. This one would be a pretty bauble."

"Listen to you, goin' all piratey on me. Bauble, jewel, treasure, next you'll be saying *Arrg.*"

"Arrg."

She laughed and bent over to splash him. They waded slowly back the way they had come. Sloane found her hand in his having no idea how it got there. It felt nice, though, as natural as breathing.

Seth scoured the drift line and picked up something that glinted. He wiped the sand and sea grime off and held it to the sun. He smiled and handed it to her. "This one's for you."

She curtsied. "Thank you, kind sir." She turned the small rock-sized creamy aqua to the light. "What did I do to deserve such a treasure?"

"This." He slanted his mouth over hers in a brief kiss. "You're a gem, too," he whispered against her lips, then kissed her again.

"Excuuuse me." She strutted ahead. "I am a sea goddess, I'll have you know, and you are my —"

"Knight in shining armor about to rescue you from Neptune's lair." He swept her up into his arms and held her above the water. "I'll save you, my little wench."

The surf came in, and she shivered when the sea mist covered her body. "You're mixing your metaphors, I hope you know."

He drew her closer to his broad chest. "I am, am I? You complainin'?" He started to let her drop.

She clung to him. "No, not me. Don't drop me."

"Can I be a knight now?" He lowered her an increment more.

Sloane shook her head, still shivering.

"No?" He moved to lower her again, then frowned. "Sea breeze too cold?"

She nodded as she trembled.

"I'll warm you up."

Seth gave her a searing kiss, and she shuddered for a whole new reason. He carried her back to the shore, set her on her feet, and wrapped her in the beach blanket.

She adjusted the blanket and wore it like a queen. "You, sir, are a knave."

"But I'm *your* knave."

"I thought you wanted to be a knight. Make up your mind. On second thought, you can be my vassal. Now, please get my royal steed."

He picked her up and flipped her onto his back for a piggyback ride. "This will have to do."

When he set her down on the boardwalk, she saw they were near their picnic spot. Joel was showing his treasures to Janie and Monalisa.

Seth walked over to the trio. "Now all you need is a treasure chest to keep it in, Joel. Your Dad and I used to beach comb when we were kids. I'll have to show you what we did and where we played pirates. It's not far from here. Up for a hike?"

Joel yelped a loud yes, which had Whaley yipping with excitement.

Monalisa stood, sounding a bit winded. "How about you guys meet us gals at the bridge? Do you mind lugging the picnic stuff back, Joe?"

Seth nodded. "It's a deal."

Monalisa waggled her fingers, singing, "Off you go, heigh-ho."

Sloane worried a tad when Seth and the children disappeared around the corner. "Joel isn't much for hikes."

Monalisa laughed. "It's a shortcut straight through the center of the island. There's a trail, a small hill, and an old overgrown willow that Seth and Whitt pretended was a pirate ship. They had plenty of duels back in the day with driftwood swords. Speaking of which, there's a place called Captain Kidd's Shipmates Adventure Day Camp that starts Monday. Janie's enrolled. Do you want to send Joel along? He might be lost with other children leaving for home and Janie away, too. What do you think?"

Sloan hesitated a moment. "I dunno . . . is it expensive?"

"Nope. I'm one of the sponsors, so it's not an issue. They have sailor-ships—"

"Say what? Sailor-ships?"

Monalisa laughed. "Aka scholarships."

Sloane winced. "Good grief, I used to be the one who—once upon a time—did the charity work. Now I'm a charity case!"

"Let me get this straight." Monalisa glared, and her tone sharpened. "Joel gets to suffer because you have your pride? Sounds to me like karma is offering you a chance to *receive* for a change." She waved a hand and continued in a calmer voice. "The day camp activities are designed to acquaint children with pirate and local history as well as their environmental opportunities. It's for kids who have experienced trauma. Seems to me that Joel qualifies as much as Janie. Besides, it's fun. Do you have something against making saltwater taffy? As boys, Whitt and Seth would have jumped at this. They'd've begged to go."

Sloane hugged herself at another mention of her husband. It still shocked her that any mention of him slashed through her like a machete.

They retraced their steps to the bridge, pausing now and then to rest, sketch, and talk. Monalisa requested most of the stops And occasionally did a little two-step before she started walking again.

Sloane looked closer at Monalisa. *Is there a balance issue?*

Monalisa chatted on, oblivious to Sloan's concern. "Seth and Whitt were as thick as Peter Pan's lost boys in Never-Never Land and just as wild. Always chasing around. Made us all nuts. They gave me most of my gray hair."

Sloane chuckled, trying to picture Seth and Whitt as boisterous boys. "They raised a ruckus, huh?"

"That they did. Took risks. Made bets and double-dog-dares. Got them in a heap of trouble, too. But nothing strengthened their bond like that rip tide."

"What do you mean?"

"They kept upping the ante. Who could do this? Who could do that? Who was the stronger swimmer? Who could top the last challenge? But one time, Whitt bit off more than he could chew and got caught in a very strong riptide."

Sloane gasped and covered her mouth. "Oh no. That must be why Whitt was overly careful on our honeymoon. On Kona, we were sharing a water mattress when a huge wave came and upturned us, and I went under. It was so scary. I couldn't see and didn't even know which way was up. Finally, the ocean threw me onto the beach. Later the mattress came back, too, but that was it for swimming on that island.

At the time, I thought Whitt had overreacted, but now I get why. I've been careful ever since. He never said much about his life, but he did go on and on about how I had to see the Cape. Funny since we never made it here . . . despite his promise to come."

"He learned his lesson then."

"Why did a simple wipeout cause such a problem? Isn't it normal, a part of the fun?"

"Whitt seriously wiped out—as in got knocked out—at Nauset Beach. Got caught in the riptide. Joe saved his life. Got him to shore. Gave him CPR, the whole nine yards. They really super bonded after that, but you must have heard that story already."

"No, not really. There's a lot Whitt never told me. Whitt seemed so, I don't know, solid . . . steady . . . balanced when we met. You'd never have known he had a reckless bone in his body. I only just learned how risky Whitt truly was when his misdeeds came to light after his death. I was struggling when we met, and he helped me get sorted. But now, I guess it's fair to say Whitt left *us* in a mess again."

Monalisa patted Sloane's hand. "How bad was it?" Her tone held sympathy.

"Real bad. The crime, the notoriety, the press. I became guilty by association. People think I knew about all of it. Believe me, it came as a complete surprise. He handled our finances. He was a financier, a financial advisor, for Lord's sake. I'm a pilot, an artist, what the hell did I know? Nuthin', that's what. And now I'm living in a shitstorm trying to get my bearings and start over."

"Whitt sent you to the right place to get things straight. As time goes on and with distance, you'll get clarity. Let yourself heal in the meantime. The salt air works magic."

Sloane shrugged and sighed. "That's my plan. God only knows what Whitt thought I'd find here."

Monalisa chuckled. "Joe, er, Seth?"

Sloane gave it a thought. "Hmm. Who knows? I first met Whitt after my mother had suffered a stroke and a car accident. She needed full-time care, but I worked to complete my degree at the same time. Whitt just sort of swept me off my feet. By the end of her life, he was handling her estate, so we were thrown together. For all I know, maybe the estate was all he was attracted to."

"Sounds to me like you are selling yourself short. Whitt talked about *his Lonnie* a lot. Pardon me, but I don't think your family had the kind of money Whitt's did. No offense."

"None taken. We had enough to keep the house. Dad had left decent life insurance. I got scholarships and student loans. We got by."

Monalisa nodded. "You took care of your mother. Finished college. Got your pilot's license." She winked. "That's a lot to be attracted to, plus you clean up nicely."

Sloane giggled. "To be honest, I didn't think much about marriage back then. I was thinking of architecture. That's why I adore *Ole Paint* so much. It combines the best of two worlds. Beauty and function. Art and reality."

"So, not in the market for picket fences, eh?"

Sloane laughed, and they walked on. "No, I was dreaming of flying high and the buildings I'd design to fill a city's skyline. My plan was to fly the skies and count the buildings I created. My mom's death and Whitt grounded me."

"But you still fly?"

"Yes. Seth and I are supposed to go up soon. Maybe I can be his partner." *Did a strange look cross Monalisa's face? Or am I imagining things?* "Wouldn't that be a hoot? Think that's what Whitt had in mind?"

Monalisa's face paled, and she reeled to the right and then centered herself. She looked like she wanted to say something but then looked skyward and threw up her hands. "Hard to say. Whitt was always thinking. I'm sure he had a plan."

"Whitt calmed the seas that were swamping me. That's why all this . . . legal mess and his death have thrown me for such a loop. He made me promise to come here and to find Joe, who turned out to be Seth, a guy I already knew. I don't know why exactly. What can Seth do? Raise the dead? Perform another miracle and make things right? I can see how coming here and escaping to this seaside heaven makes sense, but beyond that, I don't have a clue. I didn't even know who *Joe* was. I met *Seth* on my own. He was my flight instructor until my mom's illness took me back home. The rest is history."

Monalisa stilled for just a moment, but she seemed to overbalance. Recovering, she smiled and raised a hand to her head. "I remember that Whitt always said you—his Lonnie— and Joe would be good for each other, make a good team. I'm beginning to see why."

"Whitt said that?"

"Yeah, he did. He also said something along the lines of *if anything ever happens to me . . .*" Monalisa nodded emphatically.

Sloane swallowed hard. *I need to talk to Seth. Get to the bottom of this.* "Hmm. That explains Seth's savior complex."

Monalisa's body shook with laughter. "Oh, that's rich. That fits him like a rubber, doesn't it?"

Sloane chuckled and felt the heat flushing her cheeks. "That sounds about right. Second time I've heard that lately. Uh, I don't know . . ."

Monalisa's eyes gleamed. "Spoken like someone who needs to get laid or just did. Which is it?"

Sloane gulped and grinned. "I dunno. Not one to kiss and tell."

Monalisa laughed, doubling over. "I learned about that simile from Joe. Oh, sweetie, never play poker. You have a

139

tell."

Sloane's face flamed hotter. *That damn tic I can't control? Hmm.* She grimaced, then remembered the hot kisses shared with Seth not so long ago. She wondered if her lips had given her away. They had to be burned by the heat they recently experienced. Plus, she still wished she and Seth could be alone again to explore each other instead of Hamblen Island or Duck Creek's sea life. *Perhaps it's time to resume a sex life.*

Monalisa ran a finger over her chin. "*Whitt* was a bit of a savior himself, wouldn't you say? He swept you off your feet so you could live happily ever after."

Sloane bristled. "If you say so."

"You don't agree?"

With her hands on her hips, Sloane snapped her response. "Before I met Whitt, I was on my own. Taking care of my mother, going to university, then later, running a household, and raising a child. Yet I still managed to follow my passions with my art and learning to fly. I agree Whitt was a welcome reprieve and nice to have by my side. However, he wasn't my savior. My life was no spectator sport. I was managing things. It was overwhelming at times, but I didn't need a knight in shining armor. Sure, it was a struggle—"

"Oh, from what I know, Whitt respected that. I suspect Joe does, too. Perhaps he wants to lighten your load. You'll figure it out." Monalisa smirked. "I see why Whitt felt you and Joe *make sense together. You* have a lot in common. Flying is Joe's passion, like yours. He runs a business and keeps the Inn running. You're both responsible people. Plus, you're both parenting. Single-handedly, I mean."

"How did Janie end up being Seth's responsibility?"

"Not my story to tell. Ask him. He should be the one to tell you, not me."

Whaley barreled into them with the children close behind. Seth corralled the pooch and had apparently overheard

Monalisa. "I should tell her what?"

Monalisa didn't mince words. "Everything."

Seth frowned. "Not now. I have my hands full. This is hardly the place or time."

Monalisa's tone remained firm. "Tell her — or I will."

To be continued

OTHER BOOKS BY KATHY KALMAR

The Beach Series
   Beyond the Beach 1
   Beyond the Beach 2
   Beyond the Beach 3
   Beyond the Beach 4
   Beyond the Beach 5
   Back to the Beach 1
   Back to the Beach 2
   Promises on the Beach

The Mountain Series
   Mountain Hot
   Mountain Christmas
   Mountain Skye Prequel to the Weather Girls
   Mountain Kiss
   Mountain Joy
   Mountain Promises
   Mountain Holly
   Mountain Silver
   Mountain Mistletoe
   Mountain Bred
   Mountain Led
   Mountain Wed
   Mountain Hookup
   Mountain Fever
   Mountain Due
   Mountain Bachelor

About the Author

Kathy Kalmar, born in Detroit, Michigan, lives with Larry, her husband of four decades. Lately, she feels she has recovered from a sad country song life because her Smoky Mountain Tops Round House is rebuilt after the 2016 Chimney Tops II Wildfire. The residence was enlarged by four feet for the addition of their new puppy, Valentina. She is writing her next book in her new Writing Room.

She loves to read and write contemporary romance novels. Meanwhile, she remains fond of hot tubbing, chocolate, and sipping wine, mai tais, and moonshine, whether at home, Waikiki, Cape Cod, or Tennessee. Y'all come back, hear?

Contact Kathy at KathyKalmar.com
or kathykalmar@sbcglobal.net

Please feel free to leave a review on Extasy.com or Amazon.com

www.ingramcontent.com/pod-product-compliance
Lightning Source LLC
Chambersburg PA
CBHW070749120626
46557CB00002B/508